DUKES, ACTUALLY

ERICA RIDLEY

CRESSMOUTH GAZETTE

Welcome to Christmas!

Our picturesque village is nestled around Marlowe Castle, high atop the gorgeous mountain we call home. Cressmouth is best known for our year-round Yuletide cheer. Here, we're family.

The legend of our twelve dukes? Absolutely true! But perhaps not always in the way one might expect...

~

CHAPTER 1

Cressmouth, England
Down the lane from Marlowe Castle

Could it truly be considered *theft*, if the object Miss Carole Quincy intended to filch from the Duke of Azureford's summer cottage had belonged to her all along?

Carole sat on the edge of her fourposter bed to tug off her worn leather slippers. It was a brisk, late spring day with no clouds in sight, but in a mountaintop village nicknamed Christmas, 'twas best not to venture out-of-doors without sturdy boots.

Not that she was going far. Last summer, the Duke of Azureford had purchased the adjoining property. He'd be her next-door neighbor... if he were here. She was glad he wasn't. Dark tousled hair and deep brown eyes were all well and good on most occasions, but she needed to be in and out without anybody paying too much attention. She reached for a boot and yanked on the laces.

She would have retrieved her sketchbook by now, but until recently, the duke's normally vacant cottage had been housing a recovering soldier. The soldier was gone, the house was empty, the neighbors were all indoors enjoying afternoon tea... There wouldn't be a better time, but she had to act quickly.

No one knew about the sketchbook. It was the most private thing she owned. It wasn't a collection of bad poetry or "Carole + His Grace" curlicue doodles, but something even closer to her heart:

Architecture.

Painstakingly precise recreations of her house, her street, the castle upon the hill... reimagined to reflect the world she *really* wished she lived in. Happy families gathered about a supper table. The assembly rooms decorated not for lackluster "marriage mart" dances, but as a place where Carole and her friends could drink brandy and play billiards and wager their future trousseau on the turn of a card.

How she wished she could draw herself into a place where she could be herself without judgment! As talented as Carole was with architectural sketches, she was positively dreadful at capturing realistic likenesses. Instead, she copied figures from fashion plates as best she could, and outfitted each elegant lady with additional props, like flying rapiers or frothy tankards of ale.

Men enjoyed their gentlemen's clubs. Why shouldn't women enjoy equally hedonistic ladies' clubs?

"Yes, yes, because of the scandal," Carole muttered as she finished tying her second boot.

Drawing such forbidden activities was not the same as actually *performing* them, but try telling that to the gleefully shocked gossips if a single page of that sketchbook ever came to light. The moment Carole had it back in her possession, that sketchbook was never leaving her bedchamber again.

Boots on, she hopped off the edge of her bed and strode to her dressing table for the final touch.

Now where were those earrings? She shoved aside a tin of pencils and a stack of tomes on geometry and mathematics until she found the little pouch she'd been saving for just this occasion.

Two delicate gold-and-citrine earrings. She hadn't worn them in months—not since the day of the party. How could she, when she planned to say she'd lost one of the pair in the Duke of Azureford's cottage? When his butler let her in to search, she would slip her missing sketchbook back into her reticule, secure the blasted thing with a dozen sturdy knots, "find" her lost earring, and be on her way.

All she had to do was get inside.

After dropping one earring into her empty reticule, Carole fastened the other to her left ear for effect. She smiled when she glimpsed her reflection in the looking-glass. She looked positively piratical. The next sketch she'd draw would be the Duke of Azureford's cottage, brimming with fashionable ladies decked in eyepatches and—

No. This was the time for action, not imagination. Once she retrieved her sketchbook, she could daydream all she pleased. Only perhaps a month remained before His Grace would return to make use of his summer cottage. First things first.

She flung open her bedchamber door and stepped into the corridor.

Rhoda, the kitchen maid, nearly jumped out of her skin.

Carole rescued the tea tray before its contents could slide to the floor. "Is this for my father?"

Rhoda nodded. "I'm happy to take it."

"I'll do it."

Carole always took her father his afternoon tea. He rarely noticed, but that wasn't why she did it.

All right, yes. That was *exactly* why she did it. She missed her father. Missed the days when he used to take meals with her, have long fireside chats with her, do anything with her at all besides their weekly standard billiards game, which was over as soon as one of them scored twenty-one points. Of course she was as good as he was. Father was the one who had taught her to play. The game was over in the blink of an eye.

Rhoda followed Carole to her father's study and pushed open the door.

There was no point in knocking. He wouldn't notice a rhinoceros stampede through the room, much less a daughter bearing tea and biscuits. She set the tray on a table in the rear of the office as she always did and turned to face the back of her father's head.

As always, Rhoda had left as soon as Carole entered the study. Either the maid intended to give Carole and her father privacy, or she wished to politely avoid witnessing the humiliation of being no more noticeable to one's father than the motes of dust dancing before his window.

"Your tea is here, Father. Please try to eat some sandwiches."

A small grunt of acknowledgment.

Not that Carole had expected more than a swift nod. She even understood.

When her father wanted to escape life, he lost himself in his work. When the world frustrated Carole, she'd duck into a private corner and jot a quick sketch of how she would rather life be.

If she had her sketchbook at this moment, she'd draw a family taking tea together in their sitting room, just like Carole's family used to do before her mother died.

She *had* to get that sketchbook back before the wrong person found it. Not just because she mourned the loss of that particular volume, but because she didn't want the reason her father finally glanced up to be because she'd become a laughingstock. The last thing she wanted was to embarrass her father. Her goal was to make his life easier, not harder. He'd never remarried. They were each other's only relative. She wouldn't let him down.

Even if he never noticed.

Carole exited her father's study and eased the door closed behind her.

Mrs. MacDonald, the housekeeper, stood in the corridor.

"How is your sister?" Carole asked.

Mrs. MacDonald's shoulders relaxed in visible relief. "Much better, miss. Gave us a scare, she did, with those chills and all that coughing. Thank you for letting me spend the week with her."

"It was no problem," Carole said with a smile. Without much else at home to entertain her, taking over the housekeeper's duties had been a welcome way to fill the void.

Now that Mrs. MacDonald was back, however, Carole really needed to slip out of her house and over to the Duke of Azureford's cottage.

"Did you need me?" she asked.

"Tonight's menu does." Mrs. MacDonald winced. "The butcher was out of mutton, so we can't prepare the pies. What would you like instead?"

Blast. Mutton pie was Father's favorite. "Do we have fowl?"

Mrs. MacDonald nodded. "Several chickens."

"Then those will do. Thank you."

Crisis resolved, Carole made her way down the corridor and almost to the front door before her elderly lady's maid inserted herself between Carole and the door.

"Where are you going? Would you like me to plait your hair?"

Judith had been Carole's companion since birth. For as long as Carole could remember, the grandmotherly woman's favorite activity had always been braiding hair. Her own silver curls were fashioned into a crown of looping plaits.

"No need," Carole assured her. "It's not a social call. I'm just going to pop over to the Duke of Azureford's cottage for a quick moment in order to—"

"*Azureford*," Judith breathed, with the sort of giddy sigh some women used to say *Beau Brummel*. "I'm coming with you."

"He's not *there*. I don't need a chaperone."

More importantly, why was her sixty-year-old maid suddenly breathless over a duke half her age? Judith hadn't shown any interest in Azureford when he had first purchased the cottage. She hadn't even asked to come along as companion when His Grace had hosted his first and only soirée.

"Please?" Judith batted her bright blue eyes.

Something was clearly afoot, but Carole did not have time to waste ferreting out answers to mysteries. She had a sketchbook to recover.

"Fine." She shooed Judith out of the way in order to open the door. "We won't be gone five minutes. It's just a quick errand."

Carole let out a breath when she finally stepped out of her doorway and into the afternoon sun. The welcome warmth on her face perfectly complemented the scent of springtime as a cool breeze rustled the trees. It was a gorgeous day. No wonder the neighborhood children were out in the streets kicking balls and trundling hoops.

She waved at the children, but hurried down her walk without stopping to chat or play. Once her sketchbook was safely under lock and key, *then* she could take advantage of the fine weather. As soon as she reached the street, she quickly turned toward the duke's cottage.

"Carole!" a familiar voice called out warmly.

Her good friend Gloria Pringle strolled toward her, arm-in-arm with her new husband. They looked adorable together, and deliriously happy. Carole was thrilled for them.

"How is married life?" she asked, and wished she hadn't.

For years, Carole had ignored the hollow little thump in her chest every time another of her friends fell in love and started a new life. She was perfectly satisfied with her existing role as her father's caretaker. He wouldn't eat if it weren't for her. That was fulfillment enough.

"Married life is perfect." Gloria and her husband Christopher Pringle gazed at each other as if they'd been presented with a king's treasure. "We're going to go to London this year for the Season."

"You *are?*" Carole asked in disbelief. Gloria was the only other person who never went anywhere. Married life must be magical indeed if it had extracted Gloria from her shell. "That's wonderful!"

"I'm nervous," Gloria admitted, "but I can't wait to see the—are you wearing just one earring?"

Judith slid Carole a betrayed look. As lady's maid, she was responsible for the upkeep of Carole's outward perfection.

"I usually can't coax her to wear earrings at all." Judith lowered her voice. "I imagine she thinks this is some sort of compromise."

"I think it's piratical," Carole informed them. "Also, I expect to find its mate in Azureford's cottage."

Gloria blinked. "When were you in Azureford's cottage? Is he here?"

"He is not." Carole gripped her empty reticule. "And I was there for his dinner party, same as you."

"You're just now coming to fetch an earring you lost six months ago?" Gloria asked doubtfully.

This was why Carole had wanted to undertake this mission alone. Friends asked questions. The butler would not ask questions. She would just grab her sketchbook and be gone.

"She probably didn't notice it was lost until today." Judith held up a liver-marked hand to stage whisper, "She *hates* earrings. You should see the fights I must put up if I'm to get a curling tong anywhere near her—"

"It was a dinner party, not a bride auction at Almack's."

"No less a marriage mart," Judith said primly. "His Grace is single, and perhaps he wouldn't be if you would have let me accentuate your heart-shaped face with a few ringlets."

Gloria shook her head. "He's a confirmed bachelor."

"A confirmed bachelor in want of an heir and a spare," Judith pointed out. "Carole is perfectly suitable to become—"

"A broodmare?" she finished archly. "No,

thank you. Tell everyone you know that I am a confirmed spinster."

Whenever she became melancholy about not having children of her own, why, there was an entire neighborhood of lads and lasses all around her. She wasn't missing a thing.

"He *is* handsome." Gloria giggled at her husband's cross expression. "Not as handsome as you, of course."

Carole was forced to disagree. Before he'd come to town, she'd heard the same rumors as everyone else: His Grace was cold, aloof, judgmental—and handsome as sin.

She hadn't paid much attention to the gossips, but when she happened to spy the duke alighting from his stately coach... good heavens, had she paid attention! Dark hair, dark eyes, dark lashes, strong jaw, broad shoulders, impeccable everything. The entire village had skipped a collective heartbeat.

Not that Carole would indulge such twaddle. Whatever her lady's maid might dream, Carole was no future duchess. In large part because she did not plan to marry... and in equally large part because the Duke of Azureford was patently uninterested. He had thrown precisely one party and didn't speak to Carole the entire time.

"Come by later," she told her friends. "We're having pies for supper."

"We're already promised to Nick and Penelope… mayhap next week?"

"Next week," Carole echoed. "That will be lovely."

"Good luck with Azureford," Gloria called as they strode away.

"He's not here," Carole said again. Not that it would have made much difference.

His obliviousness to her presence hadn't stopped her from surreptitiously gazing at him. From her window, from their adjoining gardens, from across his mahogany supper table. Carole sighed. Dreaming about how different her life might have been was the whole reason she'd snuck off to sketch in her book in the first place. She *hated* feeling invisible.

As she was returning from the retiring room, someone bumped into her and she dropped her reticule. Carole had been the only one who saw her sketchbook fly out to skid across the ridiculously polished floor and into Azureford's library.

Before she could recover it, Swinton the helpful butler "returned" the fallen volume to the appropriately color-coded section of the duke's library shelves. Carole clenched her teeth as she turned up the duke's front path. Why had his butler even been away from his post? She should've known right then that retrieving her book wouldn't be easy.

At first it had seemed like a little luck was on her side. Azureford was leaving the next morning, thereby making it unlikely for him to stumble across her sketches. Particularly the brand new one of his front drawing room.

She couldn't dart into the library and retrieve her book in front of so many witnesses without making it look like she was nicking one of the duke's books in the middle of a party. Nor could she explain page after page of town landmarks populated by ale-swilling, cheroot-smoking ladies with snuffboxes and fashionable bonnets.

The only choice was to come back for it later. Thanks to the library's helpful color-coding, she knew exactly which shelf housed her sketchbook. She could have it tucked in her reticule in sixty seconds.

If only she could get inside.

Carole motioned for Judith to stand behind her, then gave a sharp rap with the pristine brass knocker.

The door immediately opened to reveal an older gentleman with crafty blue eyes and a tuft of white hair. Azureford's butler, Swinton.

"Good afternoon," she began brightly. "I've come to—"

Judith elbowed her way up onto the front step with almost enough force to send Carole flying into the hedges.

Swinton didn't blink.

Carole sent her lady's maid a stern glare.

Judith made no response. Her attention was completely focused on the butler.

Carole rolled back her shoulders and tried again. "I may have lost an earring in the duke's library during his soiree. Might I take a quick peek to see if I can find it?"

Swinton's blue gaze slid from Judith to Carole. "His Grace's party did not take place in the library."

True. Carole swallowed hard. *Blast* it.

"Perhaps it wasn't the library," she said quickly. "Perhaps it was *near* the library. Perhaps—"

"Perhaps you believe His Grace's household staff to be so incompetent in their posts that a lost earring would remain untouched upon the floor month after month?" Swinton inquired politely.

Carole swallowed. "I…"

...could not retrieve my sketchbook while the duke or his friend were occupying the cottage because I cannot risk witnesses.

"Miss Quincy abhors jewelry," Judith giggled. Actually *giggled*. "Such a bear when it comes to dressing up at all. I cannot let her

15

gad about town with one earring, can I? Surely a man like you wouldn't wish such mortification on a girl like me."

What in the completely-frozen-over hell was that about? Carole turned to her lady's maid in disbelief. Judith could not possibly expect a breathy little voice and schoolgirl giggles would make the duke's intractable butler—

"Very well," Swinton said briskly. "Miss Quincy has five minutes."

Carole's jaw fell open. She could practically hear her teeth click together when she forced her gaping mouth shut.

"Come on," she murmured to Judith as she took a tentative step across the threshold.

Her lady's maid let out another giggle.

Carole hooked her arm about Judith's elbow and hauled her past the butler and into the cottage.

"Are you absolutely positive you need my help?" Judith whispered between appallingly non-subtle glances over her shoulder toward the butler.

"You know what?" Carole stopped walking and dropped Judith's arm. "I have to get into that library without Swinton noticing. Do you think you can find some way to keep him near the door until I get back?"

Judith's eyes sparkled. "Absolutely."

Without a backward glance—Carole did *not* want to bear witness to whatever distraction her maid had in store for the butler—she hurried down the corridor toward the library before some other member of Azureford's staff could stop her for questioning.

She jerked to a stop just inside the library. A horrified gasp strangled in her throat as she stared at the shelves in shock.

The duke's aesthetically organized books weren't sorted by color anymore. Blue spines were not with blue spines. Red was not with red. Green was not with green. Rather than a neatly delineated rainbow, the library was a cornucopia of color, every spine contrasting wildly with its neighbor.

How was she supposed to find her sketchbook *now?*

"No, no, no," she groaned as she dashed forward to scan the shelves in search of a familiar spine.

The problem was, her sketchbook's spine didn't stand out at all. It had actually started its life as one of her father's journals. The same sort of blank journal any number of gentlemen ordered to keep their diaries or balance their ledgers. Azureford himself owned countless volumes of the same style.

The difference was, the journals that belonged to Carole's father had fancy Q embossed on the front cover. The same recognizable Q that was emblazoned on half their other possessions. If she didn't get that journal out of here during her one chance to do so, whoever stumbled across it would either immediately realize Carole had penned the sketches—or they'd think her father did. Neither was acceptable.

She hurried from shelf to shelf, yanking dark blue spines free only to shove them back moments later when their covers failed to display the family Q.

"Five minutes!" Judith called, rather… breathlessly? "Here we come! Did you find your earring?"

Carole tugged the gold-and-citrine hoop from her reticule and shoved it behind a row of books. Perhaps it wasn't a likely place for an earring to have fallen, but she needed to keep her story plausible. It could take days to find a needle in a haystack. *Weeks.*

Swinton strode into the library, his cheeks oddly flushed. "I must ask you to leave. His Grace arrives within the week, and we must ensure the house is in proper order."

"But this is his *summer* cottage," Carole stammered inanely. "It's not… summer."

This time, it was Judith who hooked her arm through Carole's and hauled her toward the door. "Thank you, Swinton. You are everything that is sweet and kind. A veritable gentleman."

"We'll be back," Carole called over her shoulder as Judith dragged her outside.

"Not without my master's invitation," Swinton replied, and closed the door in their face.

CHAPTER 2

"*A*lmost there, Your Grace."

Adam Farland, the sixth Duke of Azureford, set his well-worn sheaf of notes from the last Parliament session on the squab beside him, and directed his gaze out the window.

John, his driver, was right. A bright red sign beckoned from the rolling green grass:

Welcome to Christmas!

Most visitors flocked to England's northern-most village for the winter entertainment it usually offered. A glittering castle atop a soaring mountain, fields of gorgeous ever-greens, carolers beneath softly falling snow almost all year round. According to the latest almanac, there would be no chance of a frost fair for at least ten weeks.

A self-deprecating smile curved Adam's lips. He would not be surprised to learn he was the only resident who had timed his visit to correspond with the *least* Christmassy time of year. The already small village would hold a fraction of its seasonal population.

That was why he was here.

"Thank you, John."

Adam had purchased his picturesque cottage last year after hearing nothing but complimentary tales about this village in the House of Lords. He'd even had a few favorite pieces of furniture as well as his late father's beloved library sent up, painstakingly reassembled in the exact same manner as in the grand residence where Adam had grown up.

Neither house felt much like a home. Part of which—or, perhaps, most of which—was Adam's own fault. He loved to be around people, but hadn't the least idea what to say to them in a social atmosphere. So he said nothing at all.

Not a strategy that tended to lead to lifelong friends.

Last summer, a rumor had gone through Cressmouth that their aloof new resident would rather closet himself like a hermit than deign to speak to his neighbors. The opposite was true. To prove them wrong, Adam had thrown his first dinner party and invited everyone in adjacent houses… and then spent the entire evening glowering at his guests tongue-tied because he hadn't the least idea what to say.

This year would be different. *He* would be different.

He hoped.

"Straight home, Your Grace?"

"No. To the castle."

John glanced over his shoulder in obvious surprise. "The castle, Your Grace?"

"Please."

"As you wish."

The bustling Great Hall at the front of Marlowe Castle boasted an extensive buffet of seasonal treats, bowls of punch and ratafia, and any number of lively, cheerful locals happy to greet new guests.

That was not why Adam was going. He was replacing the comforting old library at his cottage with a brand new billiard room. The switch would force him to mingle with others rather than pass the days away by himself. If he wanted to visit his books, well, he'd have to march on over to the castle to do so, because he was donating every last one of them to the town circulating library. Well, except for a small shelf of favorites he couldn't bear to part with.

When they stopped at the castle to share the good news, Adam would have to borrow an instructional tome on how to *play* billiards because he hadn't the least idea how it was done. What mattered was that it was fashionable. If he possessed the best billiard room in northern England, gentlemen would flock to his door to play. Adam might lose every game, but he'd win friends. This would prove once and for all that "duke" did not mean "arrogant" and "shy" was not the same as "aloof."

How he'd get the word out that he possessed a shiny new billiard room in want of friendly players... well, he'd cross that bridge when he got there.

The first step was to inform the castle of his incoming donation. The second step was to pack up his father's faithfully organized books. The third step was a bit murky, but the fourth step involved basking in his newfound popularity without the slightest hint of his old social awkwardness. If he could address the entire House of Lords without tripping over his tongue, surely he could manage to make a *friend*.

"Castle coming up, Your Grace."

Spirits rising, Adam returned his gaze to the view outside his window. There went the smithy, which meant at any moment, they'd be passing Adam's cottage... Aha! There it was. Warm red brick, wide windows, a welcoming stone path to the front door.

Although there was just one road up the mountain to the castle, shops and cottages lined a half dozen narrow off-shoots. In no time at all, the cozy little homes vanished as the coach rolled to a stop before Marlow Castle's imposing front doors.

"Shall I accompany you, Your Grace?"

"Stay with the coach, please." Adam leapt to the ground. "I'll only be a moment."

Inside was an immediate assault to the senses—in the pleasantest way possible. Crackling fires, smiling faces, rows of biscuits, the low roar of conversation spiked with laughter, the sweet scent of cinnamon and nutmeg in the air. He could do this. He just needed to find someone to explain his donation to.

The only other time he'd walked through these doors had been on his first visit, just before he purchased his cottage. The welcome in the great hall was as he remembered it, but the castle was enormous. Adam knew how to find the circulating library, and that was about it.

As he glanced around, he noticed a woman just as alone as he was. She sat at a small table in the far corner beneath a sign simply reading:

FORTUNES

No one queued up, or even looked in the fortune-teller's direction. Adam's stomach twisted in empathy. He didn't believe in psychic nonsense, but he knew what it felt like to be alone in a crowd, unable to fit in.

Striking up a conversation with a turbaned fortune teller would be the perfect way to ease into being New Adam. Nothing hinged on the outcome. She would move on and he would never see her again. The meaningless exchange would be a forgettable, but important, first attempt at practicing his social skills.

Besides, how hard could it be? He'd give her a shilling, she'd give him some twaddle about luck crossing his path, and that would be that.

"No half-measures," he reminded himself. He was New Adam. This would be easy. He rolled back his shoulders and strode straight to her table.

Her turban slipped sideways as she glanced up from her glass ball.

"Sit." One long fingernail pointed at a bronze basin. "One bob for fortune."

He sat.

She stared at him without comment.

He dropped a shilling in the bronze basin.

The wrinkled, gray-haired woman continued to stare without blinking.

He shifted uncomfortably on the hard wooden chair. "Er... aren't you supposed to say something like 'love and luck will find me, thanks to the moon?'"

"Dukes, actually. Thank them."

She tapped a fingernail on the glass ball. It didn't change.

Adam refrained from informing her that she was talking to a duke at this very moment. There was no point. She likely gave the same nonsensical fortune to everyone foolish enough to hand over a shilling.

She placed both hands on the glass ball and widened her eyes dramatically. "Follow the five golden rings. They lead to your heart."

His brow furrowed. "What does that even mean?"

She covered the glass ball with a square of black silk. "It is up to you to find out."

He couldn't believe it. "I thought a fortune teller's job was to tell fortunes."

"Your job is to listen, which you are not doing," she scolded.

"Five golden rings. My heart. Dukes, actually," he parroted politely. "None of that makes sense."

"Does anything make sense? You surround yourself with fictional companions because you are afraid to make real friends."

He reeled back. "I'm not afraid! I—"

"You are comfortable before a podium because it is easier to speak to hundreds of your peers than to converse alone with just one person."

"That's not a 'fortune,'" he spluttered. "That's my *current* life. I didn't give you a shilling to tell me things I already know."

"Didn't you?" She inspected her fingernails. "Tell me, why did you invite your pretty neighbor to your party and then do nothing but stare, because your tongue is useless as wet towel?"

He stared at her in disbelief. "Do I *know* you?"

She straightened her turban. "Have you been to the old country?"

"What country are you from?"

"This one. I was born in Essex." Her accent disappeared. "If you were in search of science, you should have attended the Royal Society of Gentlemen Geologists' symposium."

He blinked. "*Is* there a Royal Society of Gentlemen Geologists symposium?"

"You want another fortune?" She pointed at the brass basin. "Two bob."

"What happened to one bob?"

"Economic instability." She tapped the basin. "Take that up with your committee when Parliament reconvenes."

"How did you know I—"

"Madame Edna knows all." She rubbed her palms over the glass sphere. "You don't wish to be seen as aloof. You are lonely. You seek the missing piece."

He dropped coins into the basin. "Two bob more. Now, how do I do it?"

Madame Edna leaned forward and lowered her voice. "Share your balls."

"Share my *what?*"

"And your table." She placed the glass sphere inside a wooden box and removed her turban. "The rest will become clear."

"Where are you going?" He placed his hands on the table. "I thought you were going to tell my fortune."

"I did." She tugged down her sign. "The rest is up to you."

With a muffled groan, Adam pushed away from her table to almost crash directly into the castle's resident solicitor, Mr. Thompson, who had aided Adam's man of business with the purchase of the cottage.

"Thank God." Adam's shoulders relaxed. "Someone sane."

"Your Grace!" Mr. Thompson said warmly. "May I help you?"

"I'd like to donate several hundred volumes to the castle library. Is there a process for such contributions?"

"There is, indeed. If the day after tomorrow is amenable, I can have several footmen and coaches available to fetch the books from your door. You needn't lift a finger."

Except for separating a dozen cherished titles Adam was unwilling to part with. "Two o'clock?"

"It's as good as done, Your Grace."

"Splendid." Adam hurried from the castle to his waiting coach before he was forced into any more awkward conversations.

"To the cottage?" his driver asked.

"*Please*," Adam replied with feeling.

The encounter with Madame Edna had proven he was not yet ready to converse with strangers. His head still hurt from the effort. He could not wait to settle into the library and relax with a favorite book. At least it was a short drive.

When his coach stopped in front of his silent, cozy summer cottage, Adam's tense shoulders relaxed. Without waiting for the driver, he opened the carriage door and stepped out onto springy green grass. Ten decorative stones up the neat front walk, and he'd finally be where he was most comfortable: alone.

As his shiny black Hessian touched the first gray stone, the wild sound of an out-of-control carriage rumbled down the hill toward him. Adam spun to face the narrow road, heart pounding in alarm.

It was not a runaway carriage. It was a high-flyer racing phaeton with a madman at the reins and three equally insane passengers crammed into the two-person seat. They caught sight of Adam at the same moment.

"It's the Duke of Azureford!" shouted a voice. "Let me out!"

The phaeton slowed to a stop, and the top of a young woman's head poked up over the side. Did the driver not intend to help her down?

Adam hurried in her direction.

Before he could offer assistance, the young woman's delicate kid half-boots landed on the colorful leaves below.

Time seemed to slow. Adam could swear his spellbound eyes registered each bounce of her golden tendrils, each magnetic sway of her hips, each crinkle at the edges of her sparkling hazel eyes.

This wasn't *any* young woman. This was Miss Carole Quincy, Adam's next-door neighbor.

His heartbeat was so loud in his ears, he barely registered the phaeton rolling merrily away, its occupants apparently confident that their recently ejected passenger could fend for herself. Nor did Adam have any doubts.

Miss Quincy was a beautiful hoyden, an unpredictable tempest disguised as spring-time. Adam's opposite in every way. She was gregarious and popular, wild and joyful, her easy manner and infectious laugh winning the hearts of every soul who crossed her path.

Adam found such disregard for decorum and proper behavior both appalling and irre-sistible. Open unconventionality might be considered an insurmountable flaw in the beau mode, but up here in the middle of nowhere, she didn't *need* to be a perfect lady. Villagers loved her because she was funny and fun, relaxed and friendly.

And now she was standing at the edge of Adam's meticulously manicured front garden.

"Lovely to see you again, Your Grace." Miss Quincy dropped a polite curtsey. "I was hoping to find you."

"You were?" Adam growled dubiously.

The growl, because he'd long ago learned it was the best way to keep from stammering or making himself otherwise appear uncomfortable with the current situation.

The dubiousness, because the last time he'd had the pleasure of Miss Quincy's company, Adam hadn't managed to speak a single word to her. Not even a growl. Why would anyone hope to go through that again?

The one and only time he'd hosted a gathering, Adam had been so tongue-tied that his guests had mostly talked with each other. Not that there had been many of them. Adam didn't know enough of his neighbors to muster up a proper *crush*. The primary reason he knew of Miss Carole Quincy was because their properties shared a border. From the wooden-latticed belvedere in his rear garden, Adam could watch her entertaining in hers. Near as he could tell, she was bosom friends with the entire village.

Except for him.

She joined him on the stone path as if they made a habit of strolling up to his front door side by side. "Marvelous day, is it not?"

"Depends if you like sun," Adam growled, then heroically refrained from slapping a palm across his overheated face.

It depended if she liked the *sun?* Who

hated the sun? Even his well-practiced growl couldn't make a comment that stupid sound intelligent.

He shifted his weight and tried to ignore his accelerated heartbeat. Everyone else could do this. Small talk about the weather was something children mastered before they left the nursery. Well, almost everyone. He was working on becoming New Adam, but he wasn't New Adam yet. He was still awkward and shy and desperately wishing she'd waited to speak to him until he finally figured out what to say.

She grinned up at him. "My apologies if my arrival startled you."

He shook his head. Admitting being startled was like admitting he was completely out of his element. "Family of yours?"

She laughed. "Le Ducs, actually."

Adam did not laugh. *Le Ducs, actually* was a mere extra syllable away from Madame Edna's prediction of *Dukes, actually.*

Was he the victim of some elaborate hoax? Embarrass the awkward duke whilst the popular set had their laugh? He'd hoped he'd left such games behind him at Oxford.

Then again, how could anyone have orchestrated the fortune teller's ruse and the coincidental timing of his arrival? Adam himself hadn't known he would be at the castle, much less at what hour. He'd made the decision to donate his books in the coach on the way up. Even his driver hadn't known until after they'd passed the *Welcome to Christmas* sign.

None of that prevented him from putting on his imperious face as they reached his front door. Haughtiness was the one mask that never failed him.

Miss Quincy bit her plump, rosebud lip. "Please excuse my forwardness, but do you mind if I come inside?

Adam stared at her in stupefaction.

"I won't bother you," she continued in a rush. "It's just, your library—"

His *library?* The place he planned to lose himself inside, in order to escape the embarrassment of not knowing what to say to others?

"It wouldn't be a good idea," he interrupted coldly. No, that frigid tone was part of his problem. Adam started again. "I cannot invite you in. I've just arrived, and I don't know in what state of readiness—"

The front door swung open.

"Welcome home, Your Grace." Swinton, Adam's beloved but maddening butler, guarded the entrance with his usual brisk efficiency. "We've been waiting for you. Everything is in order."

There went that excuse. Adam barely hid his sigh.

"Ah, Miss Quincy." Swinton took in her presence next to Adam as if he always arrived home with an attractive young lady at his side. "I presume you're here because of the golden ring?"

"The golden *what?*" Adam exploded in disbelief.

Not Swinton, too! First Madame Edna blathering on about five golden rings, and now his no-nonsense butler saying things like—

"Gold earring," Swinton repeated, touching a finger to his generous earlobe as if this new explanation made any more sense than the one Adam had imagined.

Miss Quincy's lips parted in sudden realization. "Mr. Swinton, you've had a new haircut! Subtle, but handsome. This is a splendid look for you."

It was? Swinton did? How would Miss Quincy know?

Before Adam could ask any of his questions, they were already inside the entranceway and Swinton was closing the front door.

"I'll just be a moment," Miss Quincy assured him. "I lost my earring in your library during your party—"

"Six months ago?" Adam said doubtfully.

"That's what I said," Swinton murmured.

Miss Quincy lifted her chin. "This was my first chance to come and look for it."

"Second chance," came his butler's bored voice. "You were here three days ago."

"Second chance," Miss Quincy agreed. "If you don't mind…"

But he did mind. Rather than stalk after her as she turned toward the corridor, he loped past her to block the library entrance with his own body if necessary. The library was his private domain. The rest of the world might be random and overwhelming, but his library was the one place where every single book—

Was completely out of order?

A strangled sound burst from Adam's throat as he forgot about Miss Quincy completely. His books! Who had touched them? Were they all still here? This was not how it was supposed to be at all! Adam had specifically ordered the contents transferred from his London residence to be presented in the same manner his father had kept them: displayed by size and color, making the library a veritable rainbow of literature no matter what the weather might be doing outside. It had been that way for generations. Adam would never have changed that. His servants would never have ruined the careful order. Miss Quincy...

He whirled to face her.

"Did you do this?" he demanded, his growl this time very real indeed.

"*You* didn't do it?" she countered with obvious surprise.

Of course she hadn't snuck in and rearranged his books. Swinton would have tossed her out by her ear, missing jewelry or no.

At this point, Adam didn't give a fig about Miss Quincy and her earrings. What mattered was ensuring the dozen volumes he had planned to keep for the rest of his life were still here.

If not, heads would roll.

CHAPTER 3

*C*arole leaned into a shaft of sunlight shining over the freshly ironed billiard table and carefully missed her shot.

"That was a near miss," said her father in surprise and admiration. "You almost made it."

"Thank you," she murmured in reply.

Although the le Duc family often joined the Quincys for their weekly billiards game, this afternoon Carole and her father were enjoying a rare moment together. She was taking extra care to ensure neither one of them gained too many points, in order to ensure the too-brief game lasted as long as possible. In her family, a foul shot cost two points —which erased most of her three-point lead.

"How are your sketches coming?" Father asked.

"Very well," she prevaricated.

As far as Carole knew, her best sketch-book was making the rounds with the neighbors or bobbing at the bottom of a well. The Duke of Azureford had sent her away without giving her a chance to look for it. Her chest tightened.

Father sent her a fond smile. "You'll have to let me see your drawings one day."

"One day," she agreed vaguely.

As far as Father knew, her sketchbook was full of ladylike images: still-lifes of fruit at the breakfast table, watercolors of the bright yellow rapeseed flowers in their rear garden. He considered himself progressive to allow his daughter to play billiards with a proper cue rather than a ladies' rack. If he found out she'd sketched the elegant castle ballroom as a billiard pub for whisky-swilling ladies, he'd never let Carole near a billiard ball again.

"Corner pocket." Father positioned his cue and sent his ivory ball flying toward hers, which knocked it into the bright red object ball. "Cannon. Watch out, daughter. Now we're tied."

"Twelve to twelve."

Carole bit her lip as her father took his next shot. She longed to fill the final pages of her sketchbook. If she had it, she would not draw him eager to win, but rather a score-board showing fantastical numbers high in

ERICA RIDLEY

the hundreds. After all, before each match, players agreed on how many points each type of shot was worth, and how many were necessary to win. If Carole ruled the world, games wouldn't end at twenty-one, but last for as long as the players pleased.

As she watched, her father scored two more cannons and a hazard, before losing his turn with a foul.

He grinned at her. "Seventeen to twelve. Can you catch me?"

Of course she could catch him. Carole could have won this game on her first turn.

She stalled by taking a long moment to chalk her cue's leather tip. It wasn't necessary. She'd already chalked it after every turn. But it gave her a few more moments with her father. This morning, she'd even let Judith smarten her up for the occasion. A French twist in her hair, a braided gold bracelet on her wrist, the fancy day gown she hated because the puffed sleeves' lacy trim scratched.

Father's gaze was toward the table. "What's your play?"

With a sigh, Carole eyed the green baize. Her ivory cue ball was marked with a black dot. From this angle, she could shoot... pretty much anything.

So could Father, to be honest. Part of her yearned to believe he was stretching the game out as long as possible, too. He'd never allowed her to play until after her mother died. Then he'd stopped inviting friends over. Stopped smiling altogether.

Teaching her to play had been their common ground. A way to escape the crushing loneliness of a too-quiet, too-empty house. At first, eight-year-old Carole had agreed to play because she worshipped her father—which was the same reason she borrowed his tomes on accounting and mathematics, determined to learn everything he knew.

Before long, however, the game itself was in her blood. She'd played every spare moment she could. Geometry, as it turned out, was a competitive advantage. The ability to calculate spin and angles at a glance let her make shot after shot, time after time. Billiards and mathematics had given her life purpose.

Billiards had rules the players *agreed* upon. There were no sudden surprises. No permanent disappearances. If one's ball fell into a pocket, one simply returned it into play on one's next turn.

Mathematics was just as lovely. Physics made sense. Geometry made sense. They had logic. They didn't change. They could be counted upon to always be there to help her no matter what day of the week it might be.

"Eighteen to seventeen," she said after she made a cannon and two winning hazards— and a foul to temper her lead.

"Let's see if I can fix that."

But Father missed his next shot. Carole frowned. His hands were steady as ever, but he'd squinted oddly before taking his turn.

She made a mental note to have his vision tested. Perhaps he spent all day in his study not because work overwhelmed him, but because his eyes weren't sharp enough to see it properly. Maybe all he needed was a pair of spectacles, and things would return to how they used to be.

Well, almost like old times. It had been her mother's time to go, and Carole's time to grow up and do her part. She had thrown herself into being the best caretaker for her father with the same zeal she'd given billiards and geometry.

Carole knew what that meant. She had performed the calculations. Life was like mathematics: there was a single true, perfect solution to every problem. She'd analyzed their situation a dozen ways and the answer was always to stay home. Stay a spinster. Take care of her father for as long as she still had him.

He was the only family she had left.

"Twenty to seventeen," she said after two cannons and a foul.

Father scored a cannon and a hazard before losing his turn. "Twenty to twenty. You're getting pretty good at this, love."

"Thanks for noticing," she murmured.

Before she could take her shot, a footman strode into the billiard room with a folded missive on a tray.

Carole stepped out of the way so that her father could accept his letter.

The footman held the tray to her instead.

"Whose seal is that?" Father squinted. "Wait, I know… Is that Azureford?"

It was, indeed. She lifted the square of paper from the tray with a slight tremble.

Yesterday, the duke had sent her away as soon as he saw the condition of his library, which meant he had not been the one to order the books rearranged. This was good news: He hadn't found her sketchbook. It was also bad news: Perhaps someone else had.

Carole *had* to get back in there.

Father furrowed his brow. "What does His Grace want with my daughter?"

She opened the letter to find out.

Miss Quincy,
   Please excuse my rudeness yesterday. If you

are free this afternoon, you are welcome to search
for your earring.

    Azureford

"I left something behind the night of his party." Carole refolded the paper. Her father did not ask *when* or *what party*. He paid even less attention to the goings-on outside of his house than he did inside of it. "I'll drop by to get it when we're finished with this game."

"After I win, you mean," Father teased. He surveyed the table. "Sorry, love. You haven't got a shot. This game is mine."

Irritation flashed. She was tired of being overlooked by the one person she cared about most. If Father bothered to come out of his study for more than an hour a week, perhaps he wouldn't underestimate his daughter.

Without stopping to chalk the leather tip, she yanked her cue into position. Her bracelet jangled against the wood and a carefully curled ringlet fell into her eyes, but none of that mattered. She could hit this shot with the cue behind her back.

So she did.

Her father's mouth fell open. "Have you been letting *me* win? How long has this been going on?"

She kissed his cheek. "Better luck next week."

With that, Carole lay her cue across the green baize and walked out of the billiard room. She almost even made it to the front door before the housekeeper flagged her down.

"What is it, Mrs. MacDonald?"

"I'm afraid there were no apples today at the market." Mrs. MacDonald wrung her hands. "I'll have to make pear tarts instead. Will that do?"

"Of course it will do. Pear tarts are lovely. Now, if you don't mind—"

"But apple tarts are Mr. Quincy's favorite. He eats them every evening after your billiards match."

Father ate his favorite tarts after every billiard match because Carole had arranged it that way. A delicious, cinnamon-spiced treat to thank him for not forgetting her altogether.

"Pear tarts are *my* favorite," she said to Mrs. MacDonald.

"They are?" The housekeeper frowned. "But the kitchen hasn't made pear tarts since…"

"Add a little cheese, if you would, please." Carole's stomach rumbled in anticipation. "And some walnuts, if we have them."

The housekeeper's gaze softened. "Just like your mother used to do."

Carole cleared her throat to hide the impact of those words. "Now, if you'll excuse me…"

Mrs. MacDonald hurried back to the kitchen.

Carole opened the door and strode out into the sunlight before anyone else could stop her.

She made it almost to the main road when her eyes caught sight of a happy couple strolling arm-in-arm. Penelope, and her new husband Nicholas.

Carole immediately dropped to one knee as though she were retying her boot. If she held this position long enough, they wouldn't spot her behind the hedgerow and would keep on walking toward the castle.

It wasn't jealousy, she assured herself. The pang she felt every time she saw a married couple wildly in love with each other was just… heartburn. That was it. Too much coffee with breakfast. Not a twist of longing for something she did not need and would never have. This afternoon's uncharacteristic display of temper aside, she knew her place. It was at home. With her father. He couldn't lose her, too.

After counting to one hundred, she eased

to her feet... and came face-to-face with the Skeffington twins, Annie and Frederick.

"Can we make crowns of flowers, Miss Quincy?" Annie asked.

"Bor-ing," her brother singsonged. "Hoops are better."

"All hoops look the same," his sister scoffed. "Every flower is different."

Frederick tugged at Carole's skirts. "Do you want to trundle hoops with me?"

Any other day, the answer would have been yes. Yes to flowers, yes to hoops, yes to anything. She loved children, but more importantly: when one was in want of a distraction, a pair of indefatigable ten-year-olds could be just as entertaining as a circus.

But Azureford's letter had clearly specified "afternoon." If she dallied any longer, Carole wouldn't make it before night fell. She had to hurry before Azureford stumbled across the sketchbook himself.

"Tomorrow," she promised. "Hoops and flowers, first thing after breakfast."

Before they could argue, Carole all but sprinted up the duke's stone path toward his front door.

Just as her fingers closed about the brass knocker, Judith materialized breathlessly at her side.

"How... dare you," she panted, shoving a

silver ringlet from her damp forehead. "I'm your… chaperone."

Silver ringlets? Judith had stopped to curl her hair before chasing after Carole?

"You're my lady's maid," she said firmly, although they both knew she really meant surrogate mother.

Carole hadn't been older than Annie and Frederick when the fever stole her mother away. As her father retreated more and more into himself, Judith quickly became the only constant Carole could count on.

"I was letting you rest," she added. "You said your knee was hurting because it was about to rain, and—"

"Shh!" Judith swatted a hand at her in horror. "Never mention arthritis where someone might *hear* you."

Carole rolled her gaze skyward. "Who would even care whether or not you—"

The door swung open, revealing Swinton, the Duke of Azureford's authoritative, unflappable, recently coiffed butler.

Her heart sank. He was never going to let them in.

CHAPTER 4

"*W*hy, Mr. Swinton," Judith cooed, twisting a silver ringlet about her finger. "Every time I see you, you look more handsome than the last."

Carole tensed. That was it. Swinton was going to toss them both into the street. Or the closest madhouse.

Instead, he preened—and immediately tried to hide it with a cough. "I felt it time for a new coiffure."

He felt it time for a new coiffure? What in the world?

Carole looked from her blushing lady's maid to the stoic white-haired man blocking the doorway and back again.

Oh, for the love of geometry. The Duke of Azureford's butler was flirting—or rather, carefully not flirting—with the maid Carole had known since childhood. Or thought she knew. Apparently, there was a cure for seasonal arthritis after all: The next-door neighbor's butler.

Carole flashed the letter she'd received from Azureford. "May we come inside?"

"Of course." Swinton stood to one side to allow them passage.

Carole stepped past him quickly, eager to be on her way to the duke's library.

Judith oozed into the entranceway, accidentally-on-purpose brushing her every ample curve against the increasingly flustered butler.

"You are everything that is kind and thoughtful," she fawned with a flutter of silver eyelashes.

"I was *summoned*," Carole hissed behind her hand. "He *had* to let us in."

But the truth was, Judith's not-exactly-unrequited infatuation was fortuitous indeed. Rather than hover like a mistrustful chaperone, Swinton would be too distracted by Judith's attentions to bother trailing after Carole.

In fact... A smile tugged at her lips as she inched away from them toward the library. Just because Carole had determined to live the life of a spinster, didn't mean Judith was destined to share that fate. The man had visited a *barber* on the off chance the neighboring housemaid might drop by. It wasn't exactly posies and roses, but it was as good a first step as any. If this was love, Carole wouldn't stand in the way. She—

A wall of tall, solid man blocked her path.

Carole narrowly avoided smashing face-first into his snowy white cravat. Perhaps that was why her nose hovered next to his broad chest for an extra second, breathing in the warm scent of sandalwood and spice, before she jerked backward to properly greet her host.

"Your Grace." Was that a curtsy? It might've been a curtsy. Right now, her legs felt too much like a wooden marionette to register whether she'd bent her knees or not.

"Miss Quincy." His voice was aloof and cold, just like the impression he'd always given her… until today.

After being that close to his chest, today it seemed like inside all that ice was a core of molten heat.

"Sorry about the curtsy." There. Whether she'd made a terrible one or none at all, he deserved an apology either way. "Shall we remove to the library?"

"After you." He stepped out of her way.

Carole expected to be able to breathe again, but the added arm's length of distance only meant she could see him even more clearly.

Azureford had not procured a new coiffure. His dark locks curled over his forehead with careless abandon. He was a duke, she reminded herself. He did not have to *try* to be handsome. When he rolled out of bed each morn, his black waves did their careless thing, his soulful brown eyes did their... *soulful* thing, and those gorgeous cheekbones—

"Or we can stand here in the corridor all afternoon," came Azureford's dry voice.

The library. She had forgotten.

Shoving past him to hide a fiery blush, Carole hurried down the corridor to the library. She was not Judith. She'd never been one to fawn or coo or giggle. And she wasn't interested in *Azureford*, for heaven's sake. She just happened to be awake, and conscious people found the duke's randomly inherited features handsome. Flowers were pretty, too, and she'd never flirted with *them*. This was going to be fine.

She headed straight to the first shelf and scanned the volumes in search of her sketchbook.

Azureford leaned one of his wide shoulders against the closest wall. "Are you afraid your earring somehow lodged onto the spine of a book?"

"You don't know my methods," she snapped. "Are you going to loom over my shoulder as I look?"

"Long-distance looming," he mused, his voice droll. "I had no idea that was one of my talents."

All right, fine. He was at least six feet away. Not far enough.

Carole scanned the rest of the tomes before her as quickly as she could, then turned to a different set of shelves so Azureford was no longer visible in the corner of her eye.

Too light a blue… Too dark a hue… The right blue, but not her sketchbook…

She heard scuffing from somewhere behind her. Then a thud. And another thud. Carole whirled around.

Azureford was piling books into a wooden crate.

"What are you doing?" She dashed to his side, heart pounding.

"Putting those books—" He pointed. "—in here." He pointed again.

That much was obvious. How could she stop him before he accidentally stumbled across her sketchbook?

"Can't you assign a servant to the task later?" she stammered.

"I can assign a half-dozen footmen to the

task right now." He reached for the bell pull. "Will that make you happy?"

No, it would not. Carole's hand shot out to cover Azureford's hand before he could signal his staff.

Both snatched their fingers away as if scalded.

She swallowed hard. "What's the hurry?"

"I'm donating these books to the castle library tomorrow." He arched a brow. "What's your interest?"

He was giving all his books to a public circulating library? *Tomorrow?* Her stomach bottomed in panic. If she didn't find her sketchbook in time, someone else would. Not only was the telltale Q embossed on the front cover, each illustration had been captioned in Carole's distinctive handwriting. Her curly script would give her away to any who had ever received an invitation or quick note from her—which was essentially everyone in the entire village.

The only thing worse than His Grace stumbling across her irreverent illustrations would be him donating it to a public place where anyone and everyone in Carole's village could find the sketches.

She pointed a trembling finger. "May I see those volumes?"

"I assure you, none of them are earrings."

He turned to the closest shelf and withdrew another armful of books. "Carry on with your search. I'll do mine. I need to set aside my favorites before the castle footmen arrive."

Carole's heart pounded and her chest tightened alarmingly, but there was nothing to do but take his advice. Continuing to argue would only cast more doubt on her story, and she could not afford to be tossed out. Even if it meant limiting her search to a partial set of books whilst being silently judged by the Duke of Azureford.

Maybe this was a good thing, she told herself. Azureford would be so distracted by finding the books *he* cared about that he wouldn't notice her sketchbook if it bit him on the nose.

Then again, Azureford wouldn't know which books in his collection were the ones to keep unless he was familiar with all of them. Which meant her strange little volume would stand out at first glance.

He spun toward her just as she whirled toward him.

"Let me help you find your earring," he commanded at the same time she begged, "Let me help you with your books."

They stared at each other without moving.

Carole blinked first.

"We need to document the inventory," she

babbled. "Surely you cannot mean to donate so many volumes without a master list to aid the castle librarians." Did the castle have librarians? "At the very least, an index of titles and descriptions would do. I'll help. I'm an expert on cataloguing books."

Carole was not an expert on books. She owned thirty of them, half of which were tomes on mathematics and logic, and the other half of which were filled with drawings of her own creation. She was not even an *apprentice* at cataloguing books. But she was desperate. And desperate people would clutch at every straw they could find.

"Like a ship's cargo list in the captain's log?" he asked dryly.

She nodded. Certainly. A cargo list. At this point, she'd agree to anything if it increased her chances of intercepting the sketchbook before someone else did.

To her surprise, Azureford shrugged.

"All right, Captain." He handed her a brick-red volume. "See if this works."

She opened it to the first page. It was blank. So was the second, the third, the fourth. It was a blank journal. He was saying *yes*. She hugged it to her chest.

His eyes narrowed. "That's an unusual bracelet."

Who cared about the bracelet? She glanced

down at the slender gold bands encircling her wrist. "It's several twisted together."

"Several, as in… *five?*" His voice dripped with suspicion. "Are those *five golden rings?*"

"I don't know." Why was he making a fuss? She frowned at the twisting bracelet. One two three four— "Yes, five. How did you know?"

"Because it's obvious!" He crossed his arms over his chest and glared at her. "Why are you conspiring with Madame Edna of Essex?"

"With… who?" she asked faintly.

"The fortuneteller," he said with obvious exasperation. "The one who met me at the castle and gave some fiddle-faddle about 'dukes, actually' and following the five golden rings."

"You went to a *fortuneteller?*" she repeated in disbelief.

Nothing could have proven how wrong they were for each other more clearly. Carole believed in logic and rationality. She only trusted what she could verify with maths or confirm with her own senses. And the aloof, powerful Duke of Azureford…

She stepped backward in horror. "Please don't tell me Parliament relies on *magic.*"

Azureford's fierce expression went from accusing to embarrassed to droll.

"*Essex* magic," he assured her. "The very

ERICA RIDLEY

best. Only fools trust magic from 'the old country.'"

She burst out laughing. "What other insights did this extremely reputable clairvoyant share with you?"

"That I take myself too seriously," he said with a sigh. "And probably her, too. She was my first fortuneteller."

"Will you try again?"

"Never." He gave an exaggerated shudder. "I've been a madman for two days, seeing signs where there aren't any."

"Magic isn't real."

"I know that." He wiped imaginary sweat from his brow. "Now I can go back to normal."

Normally, you don't talk to me, was on the tip of Carole's tongue. She welcomed this burst of abnormality. Or was it? Which version was the real Azureford?

She tilted her head to consider him. Logic dictated that things were often exactly as they seemed, *if* one knew how and where to look. It was a matter of simplifying the extraneous and following the pattern to its core.

Fact: At his party, the host hadn't spoken a single word to her.

Fact: At his party, Azureford hadn't spoken to anyone.

Fact: When she'd burst back into his life

unexpectedly, he'd been flustered—but he'd spoken to her.

Fact: They'd teased each other about magic. Teased, as in jokes. Like friends.

Fact: Despite her flimsy story and even feebler claim of masterful library cataloguing skills, Azureford had handed her a blank journal and welcomed her to stay.

Conclusion: The Duke of Azureford wasn't an arrogant, disdainful prig.

He was *shy*.

"You hate small talk," she said in wonder.

"I like small talk," he protested despite the immediate flash of panic in his brown eyes.

She couldn't believe one of the most powerful men in England was intimidated by something as innocuous as conversation. His party must have been hell on earth to him.

"Did the fortuneteller advise you to give away your library for some reason?"

He shook his head. "I'm putting in a billiard room."

Her mouth fell open. She had not seen *that* explanation coming. "You're swapping books for billiards?"

"Books are something you read by yourself." His gaze seemed far away. "Billiards are something that must be played with others."

Ought to be played with others, she mentally corrected. She'd long ago perfected the art of the one-person billiard tournament.

"Who are you hoping to play with?" she asked with interest.

"Everyone," he said shyly. "It's a game men and women can play. Since the game is so fast and there's only two players at a time, everyone will have to pay attention and rotate turns and…"

"…and speak to each other?" she finished. It wasn't a bad plan.

He nodded.

She could not help but like him for it. "Your goal is to make friends with… villagers?"

"My goal is… London." He set his jaw. "If I can do this here, then I can do it there."

"At the House of Lords?" she asked.

He didn't answer.

"In the *marriage mart*," she said in realization. "Of course. A man in possession of a fine billiard room is undoubtedly in want of a wife."

He didn't argue.

That settled it.

"I can help," she told him. "I know everyone in a ten mile radius. I can help you throw the best billiard party the Marriage Mart has ever seen. I even know someone who writes for the local gazette. She can pen a column that will make your party sound like the biggest crush in Christmas history."

Azureford hesitated. "In exchange for what?"

Carole blinked. She never offered to help someone in exchange for anything at all, and was a little offended he thought her so mercenary. Then again, they scarcely knew each other. And… every encounter they'd had this year had been staged on false pretenses.

Fine. His instincts were excellent. And if he was in a mood to barter, she wouldn't let this golden opportunity get away.

"Let me help," she begged impulsively.

His brow wrinkled. "You want to help in exchange for helping?"

"Not just with the party," she said in a rush. "I'm good at that, but I'd be great at designing your new billiard room."

It would be as though her sketchbooks came to life. An actual project, combining her two best talents: architecture and billiards. A match made in heaven. The first step would be—

Azureford's tone was final. "*No.*"

CHAPTER 5

*A*ll the other Chippendale chairs around his long table were empty, but Adam was not alone. He was surrounded by half a dozen stacks of detailed notes, saved correspondence, and parliamentary reports. The golden hour after breaking his fast but before the bustle of the day properly began were his most productive moments.

Usually.

Try as he might to concentrate solely on the House of Lords projects before him, part of his mind could not stop thinking about Miss Quincy. He couldn't claim not to feel at sixes and sevens in her company, but he'd had longer conversations with her than he'd had with anyone outside of the government. He had always looked forward to *seeing* her, but now he'd begun to look forward to *speaking* with her.

Not that there would be many more such encounters. They had packed up more than half the books yesterday afternoon, updating the inventory journal as they went along. This afternoon they would finish the rest, and that would be that. It wouldn't even have taken this long, had Miss Quincy not insisted on penning a cargo list for the library. Perhaps she hadn't wished for the afternoon to end, either. Perhaps that was why she had offered to design his new billiard room.

If the party hadn't been so important, Adam might even have let her explain her ideas. He knew nothing about billiards and even less about architecture or interior aesthetics. How much worse could Miss Quincy be? But he hadn't purchased this summer cottage in order to practice conversing with *one* woman. He needed this party to be perfect. The exact opposite of last year. He wanted to make friends with every gentleman, flirt—or at least, exchange pleasantries with—every lady. Which meant he needed to *practice*, so that this time when he returned to London, he'd be ready.

"Practice reading these reports," he muttered to himself. The Marriage Mart wasn't the only thing awaiting him next Season.

Adam had volunteered for the import and export committees, the Exchequer committee, and the highways and hackneys committees. He was also fighting for strict oversight of workhouses, full abolishment of slavery in all territories, and more humane treatment of the governing and custody of insane persons in or outside of asylums. Oh, and postage. Parliament couldn't seem to go more than a year or two without another Postage Act.

Most of his fellows in the House of Lords used their six months off as a welcome break. They'd think Adam peculiar for bringing his work with him on holiday. But he didn't feel like a true representative of the people if he didn't do his best to represent them all year round.

That, and being a member of every possible committee gave him something productive to do. A way to be valuable to others, even if he never quite knew how to talk to them directly.

"That's my hoop!"

"No, it's *my* hoop!"

Adam grinned to himself at the sound of children playing outside, but did not turn around to look out of the open window. He was using the natural light to reread and organize his old notes in order to create a plan for next season, and he needed to make haste. Once he finished, he had to duck back into the library to find his last few cherished vol-

umes before the castle footman came to take
all the books away.

He might have finished last night, if he
hadn't got lost in an old favorite he'd already
read at least four times.

A peal of infectious laughter floated in
with the rays of sun. It didn't sound like a
child. Adam twisted in his seat. It sounded
like—

Miss Quincy.

Of course it was. Her kissable lips and
ubiquitous presence meant nothing. Yet he
could not look away.

She was trundling a large iron hoop up the
steep road with impressive ease. A little boy
and a little girl chased after her with shining
eyes, like comets caught in the orbit of a star.
He knew how they felt. Miss Quincy had a
way of lighting up a room with her mere
presence. She was fearless and fascinating,
game for anything at any moment. Be that
spontaneous romps with children, or break-
neck phaeton rides courtesy of "le Ducs,
actually."

He rolled his eyes at the thought of the
fortuneteller. What balderdash! Miss Quincy
didn't believe in signs and neither did Adam.
He shouldn't have allowed "five golden rings"
to spook him. An earring wasn't a message
from beyond. Neither was a bracelet, no

matter how many gold bands it contained. Those were coincidences and nothing more.

His lips twisted wryly. It was a good thing she was trundling hoops made of iron, or thanks to Madame Edna, Adam's overactive imagination would think those were "rings," too.

The only reason that poppycock had got under his skin was because he *was* looking for a wife. As a duke, Adam had the responsibility to secure a respected and competent duchess, with whom he was to produce an heir and a spare to inherit the duchy. Only a very specific sort of young lady would bring honor to the title, aid his political career, and provide the right social opportunities for his future heirs.

That demure paragon certainly would not be whooping delightedly as her iron hoop flew down a mountainside at nine o'clock in the morning.

And yet.

Adam flipped to the final page of his planning journal and added a new heading to the top:

Required Qualities for my Future Wife

He dipped his quill in fresh ink and added:

Friendly
Fearless
Good with children

There. He would know he'd found the right bride when she not only possessed the proper decorum and feminine accomplishments expected by the ton, but also displayed the sort of personality Adam hoped to share the rest of his life with.

Swinton strode into the dining room bearing a silver tray.

Adam quickly shut his journal.

"Crown secrets my lord?" Swinton eased down into the chair opposite. "Or penning a love note to a future duchess?"

"Neither," Adam bit out. The heat flushing his cheeks probably wasn't helping. "Where were *you* when Miss Quincy and I spent the afternoon alone in the library?"

Swinton held out the tray of correspondence with wide-eyed innocence. "Guarding the door with my life, Your Grace. 'Tis my sworn duty never to abandon my post."

Adam arched a brow. "Even if a certain

next-door maid happened to also be inside that closed door for the entirety of the afternoon?"

Swinton leaped up from the chair and fled the room without a backward glance.

Adam shook his head. When he'd purchased this cottage and installed his lifelong butler as master whilst Adam was away, it had occurred to him to wonder what Swinton was doing in Adam's absence. If there had been only one social call during the entire summer a duke was in residence, there would have been even less for a butler to attend to without him.

Adam had allowed his friend Theo the use of the cottage for a few months while the soldier recuperated from war wounds. Again, not exactly the hustle and bustle of a typical Mayfair town house, but at least there had been someone new to welcome.

The rest of the time... Perhaps Swinton hadn't been as lonely as Adam had feared.

He placed his papers and the journal in neat piles out of the way, then reached for the new correspondence. As usual, every one of the senders served with him in the House of Lords. This time every year, Adam received a flurry of letters begging him to join this committee or head that investigation.

Usually, he said yes. He was proud of

being a good leader, and pleased that his attention to detail and command of each subject were useful to the cause. Whatever the cause. Today, he found himself wishing that just once, a letter would appear in which the only thing the sender wanted from Adam was his friendship, not his labor.

To be fair, they had tried. *Adam* had tried. He'd trailed along on pheasant hunts, shown up in his best outfit at Almack's. He'd managed to mumble something-or-other when the gentlemen gathered to boast after deer stalking, and a time or two had even participated in a minuet with some lord's daughter or sister.

Adam was fairly certain he was the only one who recalled his presence on those occasions.

The past didn't matter. He was New Adam now. Or would be soon. This billiards scheme was going to work. Whatever Miss Quincy's true motivation was for helping him with his library and his party, Adam appreciated it more than she would ever know. Soon, he would be well practiced and socially competent. Instead of just pontificating at parliament meetings, he'd develop a circle of friends and the capacity to win the hearts of ladies.

"Your Grace?"

Adam glanced up and smirked to see a footman, rather than Swinton, bearing a letter on a tray. The crafty old codger would shackle himself to the front door before returning to the dining room and allowing further questions about his interest in the maid next door.

"Thank you." Adam had been waiting for this report. It had not been part of the morning post because it had come from his man of business, who was lodged up at the castle with a hundred other travelers.

Adam despised taking meals in posting inns because he hated feeling out of place in large public dining rooms. However, according to his man of business Paterson, Marlowe Castle's enormous dining hall could not be improved upon. The kitchen and staff were second to none, but more importantly, dining services were open to the entire village.

Paterson claimed he amassed more contacts and useful information over a simple bowl of soup than he could elsewise acquire in a week's worth of hard labor.

Adam opened the report. It contained a list of commissions and the expected times to be taken for construction proposed by master craftsmen in the area capable of creating a professional-grade, visually beautiful, physically perfect billiard table. Money was no object, although he appreciated being able to compare offers.

Time was of the essence. Adam had not explained the entirety of his plan to Miss Quincy because so much of it hinged on the billiards party. If it was a success, Adam would host another and another. After all, no matter how much he practiced being bold and conversational into a single evening, one night would not be enough. He wanted to build more than just a billiard table. He wanted to support the foundation for his future matrimony.

He pulled a stack of books toward himself and opened the topmost to the first page. A handwritten dedication slanted up from the bottom:

For Azureford,
The greatest lord, statesman, and fox-hunter
England has ever known.

The inscription was meant for Adam's father. All the books he'd rescued from the crates going to the castle bore dedications similar to this one. Signed by the author, by dignitaries, by friends. Adam's father had been a legend among men. It was Adam's duty to live up to the family name.

The first step to being a proper duke was choosing the proper bride. But Adam didn't want to select some debutante willy-nilly because she happened to possess physical beauty and unimpeachable connections. That prevailing wisdom was how his parents had ended up at the altar. It had lasted only in the sense that divorce was not an option.

Neither Mother nor Father had ever been interested in the other—just what they could gain from the marriage. Her land. His title. Who cared about the rest? Once they'd produced Adam, they never spoke again. One roof; two lives. Adam refused to accept such a fate for himself *or* his future wife.

He opened his diary to the final page and added:

Must like each other!!

to the list of prerequisites. There. He had a plan. All he had to do was completely change his personality, return to London amid wild popularity, and select a perfectly pedigreed young lady in Almack's who also possessed every trait on this list.

Given all Adam was demanding of himself, four little items weren't too much to ask of his future bride, were they?

"Stop glooming," he muttered to himself. This would work. It had to. But first, he had some parliamentary notes to tidy up.

"Good morning, Your Grace," called a sunny voice. "I didn't see you there at first!"

Good God, Miss Quincy was *yelling* to him from the *side of the road*. Did she even grasp the meaning of proper behavior?

"A lady doesn't shout," he called back. "Or peek inside her neighbor's windows."

She grinned at him unrepentantly. "What are you doing? Should we finish clearing up the library?"

No. He was busy. Doing important ducal things. Taking care of Parliament and the like. His morning was rigidly scheduled, and he wouldn't have time for library antics until after noon at the earliest.

As he leaned his tailored elbow on the windowsill, he heard himself shout, "Come on over!"

CHAPTER 6

"*N*o, there is *not* time to curl our hair." Carole tried to tug her lady's maid away from the dressing table.

Judith looked longingly at the tongs. "What if I just curl *my* hair?"

"You're lucky I came back for you at all," Carole reminded her. "We both know how well you intend to chaperone."

"A chaperone in name only is better than none at all." Judith added with a wicked grin, "A bad chaperone is leagues better than a good chaperone if you're spending your time right."

Carole rolled her eyes heavenward. "I have no intention of physical impropriety with the Duke of Azureford."

"Then why did you fetch your chaperone?" Judith asked archly and swept out of the bed-room door.

Carole groaned and gave chase. "I told you. The castle footmen come today to pick up the crates. I *have* to find my sketchbook before they arrive."

"Assuming it's still there," Judith added darkly. "Maybe it's already being copied into the next quarterly gazette."

Carole slanted her a flat look. "You're not helping."

"But I will," Judith promised. "I'll keep Mr. Swinton far away from the library."

"Thank you." Carole pushed open the door and exited their cottage with her maid hot on her heels.

"If you're not interested in 'improper behavior'—which, if you've never *tried* it, is a great oversight on your part—then is His Grace the reason you walked out of the library so miffed yesterday afternoon?" Judith's eyes narrowed. "Because if he took liberties you didn't wish to give, I'm happy to stab him with a—"

"*No*," Carole said quickly before some passer-by overheard and the entire town began speculating. "I was vexed because he rejected an offer without listening to me, but I can't blame him. He's a duke and I'm a nobody. He probably has a team of architects and craftsmen locked in his guest room for whenever the urge to renovate strikes his fancy. He doesn't need *me*."

Judith's concern melted into a knowing smile. "So you *do* like him. Mmm, all that rugged, ducal power."

"He's nice," Carole replied primly. "He's more complicated than I first imagined. And funnier."

"The Duke of Azureford has a sense of humor?" Judith said with obvious skepticism.

"You'd already know the answer to that if you were ever in the same room as him," Carole pointed out. "Now hush. We're here."

Before she could reach for the brass knocker, Swinton opened the front door.

Judith immediately simpered, "Why, Mr. Swinton, surely it's a crime to be more handsome every day than the last."

Carole marched past them into the corridor before her tender ears overheard whatever the butler planned to murmur in reply.

Azureford was still seated at his dining room table, his back to the open window. When he caught sight of her, he glanced up and smiled.

She felt that smile all the way to her toes. It wasn't just a curve of those wide, firm lips, but a full-body smile that relaxed his posture and lit up his handsome face as if he'd spent all morning hoping she would walk through his door.

The silly smile spreading over Carole's face no doubt mirrored his reaction.

She cleared her throat. "What are you working on?"

"I can put it away." He started to stack a pile of journals.

"I don't mind." She stepped into the room. "Are you redoing the inventory list?"

"And risk dismemberment? That's your domain." He lifted a sheaf of documents. "These are House of Lords projects."

"*All* of this?" She moved to take the seat opposite him, but he motioned to the empty chair at his side. Soon, their elbows were touching. "I thought you were finished for the summer."

"Parliament closed in July and the new session won't reopen until November, yes. But there is always work to be done. These two journals chronicle the changes in imports and exports, this pile of correspondence has to do with choosing leadership for a few committees, and this stack of reports—but of course I'm boring you."

She shook her head. "You're not. Really. The first book I ever read twice was a tome on descriptive geometry, so if you'd like to make a wager on which one of us is more likely to out-bore the other..."

"Ooh, descriptive geometry," he echoed with wide eyes. "Is that one by Radcliffe or Walpole?"

She swatted his arm. "Gaspard Monge, actually. Perhaps more people would read those gothic novels if they applied more logic than swooning virgins and dark fantasies."

"No they wouldn't." Azureford affected a dramatic pose. "'I must flee the Castle of Otranto with its ninety degree angle flying buttresses.'"

"Well, that explains why the castles are always so frightening," she replied with a straight face. "Buttresses cannot properly support their weight unless they're installed at forty-five degree angles. A good, solid swoon is completely understandable when there's a castle falling down about one's shoulders."

He laughed and opened the journal marked *Imports*. "Remind me never to buy you a romantic novel."

Carole stuck out her tongue and listened to his explanation about the intricacies and differences between the Importation Act of 1812 and the Import Act of 1813.

In no time, she began to realize that Azureford was not only surprisingly humble and droll, but also very, very clever. He scarcely needed to glance at the journal entries to quote them exactly. How many times had he gone over this material? Could he just look at things and remember them? No wonder everyone in the House of Lords seemed to want him on their committee.

Luckily for them, Azureford seemed passionate about every one of the worthy causes blanketing his dining table. If he hadn't been a lord, Carole rather suspected he'd have served in the House of Commons. Being born a duke was essentially *carte blanche* to do or have anything His Grace desired, but he wasn't resting on inherited laurels. He was probably the single most competent representative in all of Parliament.

She shifted in her seat. This new facet made him all the more attractive.

Not that she dared develop a *tendre* for him, of course. He was shooting for the stars and she was staying put. No matter how magnetic she found his passion, her loyalty was to her family and the vow she'd made never to abandon her father.

Well, that was putting the cream before the scone, wasn't it? Her cheeks heated. She was here as his library inventory consultant, not to compete as a future bride.

He paused. "I've lost you. What are you thinking about?"

"Parliament," she hedged. *You being wrong for me in every way.*

"I don't mind. Most people see it as an excuse to come to Town for the Season." He winced as he belatedly realized most residents of this village might not share that privilege. "Oh. Have you ever had a... Have you been to London?"

"No and no," she answered, for the first time wondering how different her life might have been, had she made different choices. "I have a great-aunt who would have been willing to sponsor me for a proper come-out, but my place is here."

"You could be part of Society," he said with astonishment, "but you said *no?*"

"It's... I couldn't leave my father. You didn't see him after the fever took my mother. I mean, you don't see him now, but back then it was even worse. He was too melancholy to rise from bed, to dress, to eat. If it hadn't been for me, I think he would have died of a broken heart. I couldn't leave him and risk the melancholy returning. Not when there would be no one to save him this time."

"I am sorry," Azureford said softly. "I do not know what it was like to be in your situation, but I do know how it feels to lose one's parents. I would not wish it on anyone."

She pushed up from the table with a forced smile. "Weren't we meant to finish packing up the library?"

"Of course." He rose to his feet, but his dark gaze stayed locked on her. "After you."

For the next hour, the only words spoken between them related to the titles she was adding to the master list, or the books Azureford swiped from the crates and carried over to his stack of rescues.

Carole was just about to tease him about keeping Edward Gibbon's *Critical Observations on the Sixth Book of the Aeneid*, when she finally caught sight of a familiar blue journal with a distinctive Q embossed on the front cover. She wrenched it from the stack and pressed it to her pounding chest with a disbelieving gasp. It was here. She'd found it!

She resisted the temptation to flip through its pages at once, raking her eyes over her reimagined renditions of local landmarks and private parlors. It was as if a part of her heart had finally been returned. The part that believed escaping into a false reality was just as good as living in the real world. She started to tuck the sketchbook inside her reticule before Azureford noticed anything amiss, only to realize he was staring right at her. Her stomach sank as she slowly turned to face him.

He raised his brows. "What did you find?"

"M-my missing earring?"

"It looks surprisingly like one of my books."

"Not your book." She took a deep breath. "*My* book."

He crossed his arms, one eyebrow cocked expectantly.

There was no good way to do this, so… out with it all at once. She held the sketchbook flat and upended her reticule. The "missing" gold-and-citrine hoop tumbled out, winking accusingly from atop the dyed leather.

"You lost your earring," Azureford said slowly, "inside your reticule?"

"I lied," she admitted, although it was obvious he'd worked that much out for himself. She put her earring back into her reticule and lifted up the sketchbook. "I lost this on the night of your party."

His eyes were unsmiling. "A diary of your innermost thoughts?"

"Pictures of them," she admitted. "It's a sketchbook. I wasn't going to show you, but I thought you might like—"

"—to know the real reason you've been

visiting?" A muscle worked at his jaw. "Yes. Thank you for telling me. You can go now."

"No, it wasn't like that at... All right, yes. That was the reason I visited *this* year. But I came to your party last year because I wanted to get to know you better, and I still do. You're not at all what you first seemed, and I like you so much more than I imagined I would."

"This apology of yours," he said dryly. "It needs work."

"I want to help," she burst out. "That's what I'm really saying. Judith is the only other person who knows this sketchbook exists, but no one but me has ever seen the drawings. I love buildings. I love imagining how I would remodel them even more. I drew your parlor—"

"You drew my *parlor?*"

"—when I dashed off to the retiring room for a few minutes. On my way back, someone bumped into me and my sketchbook skidded into your library. I didn't want to look like I was stealing one of your books, or call attention to its contents..."

"You drew my parlor in 'a few *minutes?*'"

There was only one way to prove to him that she possessed the skills he needed most. Carole took a deep breath. She was going to have to trust him. A little. And hope that the

ERICA RIDLEY

duke's infamous hauteur and reticence meant he was much too proper to gossip—not that he had close friends in town to share scandal-broth with anyway.

"Here." She ignored the shaking of her hands. "I'll show you. It's the last one. It's unfinished." She flipped to the right page and shoved the sketchbook in his direction.

After an agonizing moment, he stepped forward and accepted the small volume. He studied the illustration in extended silence before finally looking up. "Why is my parlor filled with drunken, cheroot-smoking women?"

"They're not drunk," she protested.

"They're carrying tankards of ale and flintlock pistols. At any moment, one of them is going to slur, 'I wager I can shoot that bonnet right off of your head' and the next thing you know, there'll be a bullet hole in my favorite framed kilt."

"You have a favorite kilt?" she stammered.

"Apparently. You've drawn one on my wall." He held up the sketch, eyebrows raised.

"I was going through a Scottish phase." She waved a hand. "But if you take away the pistols and the cheroots and the extraneous kilt, this is exactly your parlor. Not how it *does* look, but how it *could* look."

"If I were insane," he agreed. "What's your point?"

"My point is, I can do this. I can turn your library into a billiard room."

"Anyone can turn a library into a billiard room. Step one: Get rid of the books. Step two: Install billiards. I've already received estimates from the best craftsmen in the area."

"Anyone can purchase a table," she parroted. Good God, he needed her far more than he knew. "Not everyone can create an *experience*. The best table your money can buy might be the centerpiece, but that doesn't mean just tossing it in the middle of the room."

"It doesn't?"

"No! Have you even played billiards? Lighting is fundamental. Daytime play is best with natural illumination. Evening play requires a custom-crafted framework of three to six oil lamps positioned at the proper angle."

He nodded. "I remember. Ninety degrees."

"That was buttresses, not billiards. Receptacles will catch the oil so that it doesn't fall onto your freshly ironed baize, and the cabinetry to house your cues, maces, and ball box need to—"

"May I?" Azureford's finger hovered just beneath the prior page.

Carole sighed. She could recognize a *no.* "Please do."

Her skin crawled with invisible ants as he slowly paged back through each drawing. Occasionally his lips would quirk or a brow would raise, but he otherwise kept his silence.

"You want to do this the right way, don't you?" she burst out when she couldn't stand the anticipation any longer. "You said I could help you with your party. Let me *help.*"

He glanced up from her sketchbook. "How?"

"Look." She flipped the inventory journal to a blank page and started to draw. "These walls have a fixed height and length, don't they? The fireplace is *here,* and the windows are *here* and *here.* We'd rip out the shelves. Presuming cabinetry like… *that,* and a billiard table like… *that,* then this is a rough approximation of how I would alter this room to maximize its attributes."

The duke exchanged her sketchbook for the inventory journal.

She tried to make him see. "You dream of making the best possible impression on your future duchess, and I dream of being allowed to do a project like this just once in my life. To design and decorate as I see fit. This isn't only our best attempt at making your billiard room be all that it can be, but each of us, too. We'll grant two wishes at once. Not bad, is it?"

Her heart twisted. He was going to say no. He was still angry about her deception. She had one chance to resolve this. No matter what it took.

"Help me help you..." She took a shaky breath. "...to marry someone else."

*a*dam sat in the dappled sunlight of the wooden-latticed belvedere in his rear garden and tried to escape into the book in his hand. It was no use. He moved a ribbon to mark his page and glared at the pretty flowers blooming in the Quincys' garden.

He could be disappointed that Miss Quincy's sudden interest was due to ulterior motives, but he couldn't be angry at her. He'd had ulterior motives of his own, did he not? Realizing he'd wished to "practice" with the entire village before removing to the Town he *really* cared about could not have been any more complimentary than learning the only reason Miss Quincy kept coming over was to retrieve her sketchbook.

Truly, what if anything, had changed? Earring, sketchbook, billiard room... She still wanted something, and so did he. If she could help him reach his goal rather than flail at it awkwardly, what sort of fool would refuse the offer?

He removed his House of Lords diary from the basket by his feet and flipped to the final page. With a pencil, he added:

Honest
Reciprocates feelings

to the list of required qualifications for his future bride. He didn't have feelings *yet*, but he was annoyed enough with himself and Miss Quincy to imagine how badly he would have felt if he fell in love only to discover the woman he hoped to make his wife was only waltzing with him because it cured her indigestion or some such.

He tossed the pencil and journal back into the basket along with his book. Reading was no good. What he really wished he had his hands on was that sketchbook. He'd only recognized a handful of places—his parlor, the castle entrance hall and the circulating library —but he suspected most of the village had found its way into her little book. With different dressing, of course. Every single scene seemed to involve riotous women making any number of dramatic choices.

For someone as outgoing as Miss Quincy, she'd certainly managed to hide an intense inner world.

"There you are, Your Grace." Swinton swept into view with a large silver tray, which he placed upon a small wooden table inside the belvedere. "Biscuits, lemonade, and a note from Mr. Paterson."

Adam's man of business. He reached for that letter first before the lemonade.

Your Grace,

I've shown the sketch to architects and builders as you requested. Other than enlarging the windows as seen in the illustration, most of the changes are cosmetic, and as such, not structural engineers' particular strength. They all seemed to find it as fine a suggestion as any.

I took the liberty of sharing the drawing with the same craftsmen who provided proposals for the billiard table. They exclaimed over the use of light, the recessed cabinetry where the library shelves once were, and the intricate lighting system. The design is brilliant. One workman even claimed the billiard table in the drawing almost perfectly matches the design and dimensions of the table in his proposal, making it a perfect match.

I enclose the sketch. Please advise.
Paterson

Adam fished in the basket for the report containing the craftsmen's proposals, and flipped through them until he found the one his man of business had referenced. It had been provided by John Thurston of Catherine Street in London. Not a local laborer at all, but England's most renowned maker of billiard equipment, according to Paterson.

According to Miss Quincy, too, by the look of it.

He didn't have to check his notes to know that choosing London's most celebrated expert would exponentially increase both the cost and time required.

But as Miss Quincy had said—he wanted to do this the right way. To make the *best* impression. The last thing he needed was to have his guests standing about talking about how stingy he'd been with the materials or how much foresight he'd failed to give the question of lighting. Which he hadn't even *known* was an important question to ask until their argument.

Whatever flaws she might possess, one thing Adam couldn't help but admire was her willingness to *try*, no matter how unlikely the

ERICA RIDLEY

chances seemed for success. What would happen if he set her up to win? He was Project Billiards committee *leader*, not the entirety of the committee. With his resources and her expertise, Adam's billiard room would not simply be a nice touch, but possibly the talk of the town. In a *good* way.

He drew out the journal one more time.

Knows what she wants
Does everything she can to achieve it

"I just need one more!"

"Hold on, I'm getting it."

Adam shut the book and stared through the lattice at his neighbors' garden.

Miss Quincy stood near a waist-high row of blooming rapeseed with a pair of shears, talking to one of the little girls that lived nearby. Both wore crowns of bright yellow flowers atop their heads and matching yellow necklaces at their throats. In the little girl's outstretched hand was a fifth loop of braided flowers.

"Five golden rings," he growled in disgust. "You're bamming me."

As if she'd heard him mutter, Miss Quincy

glanced up and met his eyes. Rather than shouting to him as she might once have done, she gave a tentative little wave.

"When you're done dusting yourself with pollen," he called out, "meet me in the library."

Although he was too far away to discern the sparkle returning to her eyes, Adam swore he could *feel* them twinkling at him.

"Five minutes," she yelled back. "This band is for Annie's father."

Annie held it aloft as though the ring of yellow flowers was the Crown Jewels for a king.

"The finest rapeseed headwear I've ever seen," he assured the little girl as he exited the belvedere with the basket on one arm.

She gave him a gap-toothed grin.

Adam entered the library and began organizing the basket's contents back into their neat piles. General correspondence, House of Lords, Billiards Committee. He had barely finished when Miss Quincy burst through the door.

He spun toward her. "What happened to five minutes?"

"It's been ten." She glanced over his shoulder, not at the table but at the lone stack of books on his otherwise empty shelves. "Those are your can't-live-withouts?"

He lifted a palm in acquiescence.

ERICA RIDLEY

She ran over to the books to inspect the titles. "If these are your favorites, why are they in such terrible condition? If you bent the page-corners of one of *my* books, I would smite you with a plague of locusts. Or spiders. Whichever you hate the most."

"They aren't my books," he admitted. When she spun to face him with a question in her eyes, he explained, "They belonged to my father. They're his favorites. We used to argue about cracking spines and bending corners, but now those flaws are the things I love most about those books. It's proof he lived, he loved, he was happy. When I touch them, it feels like he's still here."

She touched a hand to her chest and gave a tight nod. "I know what you mean."

He leaned against the table. "That's not why I summoned you."

"Is it because you're in the market for a rapeseed crown?" she guessed. "I know a girl. We can arrange it."

"I know a girl, too." He corrected himself, "A woman. Some might say, an expert in designing the perfect billiard room."

Her hazel eyes widened. "Who says that besides me?"

"Me." He lifted the most recent letter. "And Paterson, my man of business." He brandished the winning proposal. "And some fellow called John... the Worst? John Thirsty? John—"

"John Thurston said *I* know how to design the perfect billiard room?"

"I watched you make that sketch in less than fifteen minutes, and you managed to include a billiard table that was recognizably one of his. He won the proposal. Of course he thinks you're brilliant."

"John Thurston is going to build you a custom billiard table?" Her expression went from shocked to overjoyed. "*Here?* In Christmas?"

"Right there where you're standing. I don't know if you're still interested in helping me remodel this dusty old room—"

"*Yes!*" She grabbed his hands and danced around him in an excited circle. "I could kiss you for this! It's a dream come—"

His heart thumped.

Her cheeks went scarlet, as if just realizing what she'd said. "I didn't mean..."

He wished she *had* meant it. There was suddenly nothing he wanted more than to pull her forward into his arms and lose himself in the taste of her lips.

"Well, then." He forced himself to let go of her soft hands. "Let's get to work. I'll only be here for another month."

"A *month?*" Her voice cracked "To tear out

your old library, put in a billiard room, search for, interview, and employ fast, capable construction personnel, turn a haphazard sketch into actual, beautiful cabinetry, commission balls and cues and maces, somehow squeeze into the schedule of the most sought-after billiard table artisan in England... This will take *several* months."

"Nothing to it." Adam had faced far tougher deadlines in the House of Lords. He could succeed. *They* could succeed. "Billiards party in four weeks."

CHAPTER 8

*C*arole hopped across her bedchamber rug as she tied her final boot. Every person in her household had needed her help this morning, and now she was running late to Azureford's.

True to his word, the indomitable man had summoned draftsmen and journeymen out of the ether. Over the past week, a flurry of artists and experts had paraded in and out of his cottage, and Carole had been right by Azureford's side through all of it. They'd spent long hours deliberating over designs and materials and proposals.

Today was the day the actual renovation was set to begin. Carole didn't want to miss a single moment.

She skidded out her bedchamber into the corridor and nearly crashed into a maid carrying her father's breakfast tray.

"Shall I take this to Mr. Quincy, miss?" Rhoda asked.

Every other morning, Carole's answer to this question had always been, *No, I'll do it.* Even though her father barely glanced up from his desk, at least he would know his daughter never stopped caring about him. The who-takes-the-tray dance was part of the ritual.

"Please do." She curled her fingers about her reticule. "I must hurry."

"You said... yes?" the maid stammered in obvious surprise. "That is, of course, miss. I'm happy to."

Carole was always happy to, too. This uncharacteristic deviation was temporary. Soon enough, Azureford's holiday would end and the Quincy household would resume its predictable patterns.

"Thank you, Rhoda." Carole swept out the door before the maid's shocked eyes could ask any more questions.

When all of this was over, she'd dedicate even more time to Father to make up for her absence. If it weren't for Carole, he'd never come out of his study. Perhaps if she did more for him, he'd have free time... and spend some of it with her.

Before any early morning passersby could stop her, she sprinted from her front door to

Azureford's. It was wide open. Men in frequently patched work clothes streamed inside, or wandered around to the rear to squint at the pair of decorative windows Carole intended to replace with large, sunny panes to let in more light.

Inside, the chaos was perfection. The level of noise and the impossibility of walking in a straight line without bumping into someone made her feel like she was in the middle of Marlowe Castle's ballroom at the height of the Christmas season.

"I need a measuring tape," called out one of the men.

She yanked hers from her reticule and slapped the coiled white ribbon into his outstretched hand.

He grunted in response and climbed back up his ladder without a single word of thanks.

Carole's spirits soared. She had never felt so much a part of something in her life. He hadn't said, *Wot, a woman?!* or tried to explain in gentle terms that the very competent men were doing very important things right now, and maybe the little lady would like to retire to a pretty drawing room and mind her embroidery while they did the real work.

"Got a hammer and nails in there, too?" came a low, amused voice.

She spun to face Azureford, her heart pounding in excitement.

His dark brown hair tumbled across his forehead, as though he'd been up for hours. However, his polished black Hessians, tight-fitting buckskins, gorgeous jay-blue coat, and sharp white cravat made him look as if he'd been planning an outing with the *beau monde*, rather than a fortnight of sawdust and upheaval.

"All these big, strong men, and none of you thought to bring a hammer?" she teased.

His dark eyes narrowed as though he hadn't liked the idea of her looking at other men. Her stomach fluttered in response. She could never tell him that the room could be filled with a thousand strapping dukes, and her gaze would still only be drawn to him.

"We're about to find out if your plan will bear fruit." His serious expression reminded her what they both had at stake. "Ready?"

Voice mute, she gave a jerky nod. She'd taught herself mathematics. Bested her father at billiards. Become head of her own household at nine years of age. She was capable of *this*.

"Good. Tomorrow, the woodworker arrives to take final measurements for the cabinetry you designed." Azureford gestured behind him. "Today, we destroy perfectly sound shelves in order to make room."

"No destroying!" She choked in horror. "You don't need those shelves anymore, but the wood can be repurposed. Donate it to the castle if you haven't any use for it yourself, and they'll see it finds a worthy home."

Without question, the Duke of Azureford turned and barked new orders to the men behind him.

They gestured their understanding and began stacking a pile of serviceable slats where the desk had once stood.

Joy threatened to overtake her. She looked around in wonder and pride. This wasn't just another wistful sketch from her imagination. This was really happening. Azureford's vast wealth and preternatural efficiency had turned her ideas from a sketch to reality in what felt like mere seconds.

Over the past week, she'd witnessed firsthand what it must be like to work alongside him in the House of Lords. No wonder everyone wanted him on their committees. He saw the big picture and the small details. Wrangled paper and people and projects without blinking an eye.

Carole's eyes didn't stop blinking from the dust flying in the air and the intermittent bang of hammers. The furniture was gone from the library, the workers were ripping shelves from the walls, and a team on the outside of the cottage were climbing up ladders next to the windows.

An older man in a battered cap drew up next to Azureford. "Need your approval for the changes to the design, Your Grace. Jimmy says—"

"Not me." Azureford's fingers grazed Carole's arm. "Talk to her."

Her chest thumped.

"Here." The man shoved a sheaf of papers into her hands and jabbed at the topmost one with a dusty finger. "Them cabinets look pretty enough how they be, but Jimmy says if we make 'em a set of three and build back further into the wall…"

Carole nodded her comprehension as they went through each drawing. Her original design had been reworked several times to represent all angles. She'd been considering the cabinets from the perspective of someone standing inside the room, but now that the bookshelves were gone, they had a new understanding of how much extra space had been built between the back of the shelves and the outer wall. Jimmy's idea was a good one.

"He's right," she said eagerly, and fished a pencil from her reticule. Using the closest wall as a writing surface, she sketched new lines on top of the old ones. "If we increase the depth to that, and restructure the doors like this…"

"Aye. Hmm. I see. Jimmy, get your boots over here!"

The next few hours passed in a whirlwind of explanations and activity. Noon had come and gone before Carole realized she'd been on her feet for so long she could no longer remember breakfast. She didn't care. Let her stomach rumble. She was having the time of her life! She'd *live* in this room if need be until it was perfect.

"Come on." Azureford looped his arm through hers and all but dragged her out of the library and into the dining room, which had become their makeshift base of operations.

She stumbled when she glanced over her shoulder toward the construction. "I—"

"—have to eat," he finished firmly, and pulled out a chair for her.

Instead of their usual disarray of documents, the table overflowed with an abundant tea setting.

She sat, suddenly famished. "Thank you."

Rather than preside from the head of the table, he took the seat beside her, as had become their custom.

"Pear tarts." He placed two on her plate. "Not another word until you've eaten them."

She grinned and picked up her fork. From the moment Azureford had discovered pear tarts were her favorites, tea hadn't been served without them. Enjoying two at a time was no hardship at all.

When tea was finished, she turned to Azureford as the footmen cleared the table. "I was thinking..."

He held up a finger as if he'd been expecting precisely those words, and retrieved a small box from a side table. She laughed as he displayed his treasures: three new journals, two freshly cut plumes, and a large bottle of ink.

"I don't think *that* much," she teased him.

He arched his brows. "If I don't keep my eye on you, all three of those journals will be fully illustrated by nightfall."

"Then I suppose you better keep your eyes on me," she answered lightly.

His voice turned husky. "I do."

Her pulse skipped. Suddenly very aware of how close their bodies were to each other, she busied herself with the plumes and journals.

The moment passed, and in no time their heads were bent together over the designs for the billiard room and the timeline they needed to adhere to in order for all the pieces to fall into place on schedule.

Carole was no longer certain which were her favorite moments of the day: standing in the eye of the construction storm, or being elbow-to-elbow with Azureford amid a blanket of plans and sketches.

Despite being a powerful duke, he was neither arrogant nor imperious. He listened to her suggestions as though she were the one with the Oxford degree. Not that he hid his own opinions. Azureford was splendid to debate ideas with. His analytical nature was the perfect complement to her artistic imagination. Rather than argue, their conversations were liberally sprinkled with *what if we* and *oh, I hadn't thought of it that way!*

They weren't just a good team, she realized with wonder. Over a solid week of near-constant togetherness, they'd managed to become *friends*. She was free to be herself. Draw what she pleased, make as bold a suggestion as she liked. And as for him... what more could a woman want?

"This week," he continued, "Thurston's workshop is crafting the pieces for our billiard table. Next week when it arrives, they'll install it directly in the new billiard room—"

"I'll get to meet John Thurston?" she squealed.

"A pox on Thurston," Azureford scolded with mock jealousy. "You'll meet his contracted assembly team and that's all."

She feigned a lovesick swoon. "I'll meet someone who has met John Thurston!"

"If I never hear that name again…" Azureford growled.

"Miss!" Jimmy poked his head inside the dining room. "Campbell wants to know if we can—"

"I'll be right there."

She leaped to her feet to gather their papers. Belatedly, she realized she must have set her teacup atop one of her sketches instead of in its saucer, for it had left a telltale golden ring around part of her signature.

Azureford was staring at it as though the stain foretold certain doom.

"Sorry." She shuffled the sheet to the bottom of the pile. "I'll draw a new one. Let's go and see what Jimmy wants."

When they reached the billiard room, she saw they'd finally completed the one modification she hadn't yet shared with Azureford: a reading nook in the corner near the fireplace, with room for a chaise or sofa and a place of honor for his favorite books.

His jaw dropped. "Is that… Did you…"

She nodded. "The best light is supposed to be for the billiard table, but I know how deeply the old library kept you connected to your father. All his books are there, with room for more. You can hold them and read them anytime."

His dark gaze swung to her and he stepped close enough to almost touch chest-to-chest. "The only thing I want to hold right now is…"

For one mad, dizzying moment, she almost thought the Duke of Azureford was going to kiss her. Right here. Right now. Amid the clanging of hammers and the tickle of sawdust and in front of a dozen burly witnesses. Carole wouldn't have stood there and let him kiss her.

She would have kissed him back.

CHAPTER 9

The door to Azureford's summer cottage swung open. With a sweep of his arm, Swinton welcomed them inside.

"*Please,*" Carole begged, keeping her voice low so only Judith would hear. "I know I told you that first day to keep the butler distracted elsewhere, but if you don't physically restrain me from throwing myself at Azureford, God only knows what embarrassing thing I'll… Judith?" Carole glanced over her shoulder in disbelief. "*Judith?*"

Both her maid and the butler had vanished into thin air as though the entranceway secretly concealed a trap door.

"Fair-weather chaperone," Carole muttered under her breath.

She would have to keep her desires in check herself.

It shouldn't be *that* hard. As long as she

kept reminding herself that everything she and Azureford did was so that he would have a better chance of landing the diamond-of-the-first-water Society bride of his dreams. A fortnight ago, he'd told her he would only stay another month. He had an agenda to keep. The clock was ticking.

She strode into the billiard room with her heart under lock and key and her head held high.

Azureford was there waiting. He lounged on the satin-trimmed sofa in his reading nook with absolutely no regard to the wrinkles forming on his olive-green coat or the dent his chin was making in the folds of his cravat. When he saw her, his eyes lit up and he tossed the book he'd been reading aside.

Her heart melted a tiny bit.

He leaped to his feet, palms outstretched at his sides. "What do you think?"

About him? Gorgeous. Brilliant. Temporary. But she knew what he meant. By now, they barely needed to do more than make significant eye contact for the other to understand the meaning.

As of last night, construction was complete. This was the first morning without renovators everywhere. The billiard room contained absolutely everything but the billiard table. She stood in the center where the table would soon be and turned in a slow circle. The windows were large and sunny, the gilded cabinetry was intricately carved and its contents well-stocked.

In addition to the reading nook's plush sofa, comfortable guest chairs dotted the perimeter of the room with small round tables between for spectators to set their canapés or glasses of champagne while they awaited their turn to play.

"It's beautiful," she admitted. "Your party is a foregone success."

"*You're* the secret to my success. I would've purchased the best table local carpenters could cobble together, but I wouldn't have *this* —" He gestured at the cabinets, at the reading nook, at the bright windows illuminating his smile. "—without your help. Thank you."

"You're welcome," she mumbled, suddenly unsure how to take his praise. Was it just a compliment? Or was the subtext that they were finished now, and she should go home?

He pulled a small blue volume from the reading nook. "You left this behind. Don't worry, I wasn't going to keep it."

Her sketchbook. He had placed it on the shelf where he kept his favorite books.

Cheeks warm, she accepted the worn volume. "I wanted to add one more illustration."

"I know." His twinkling eyes were unrepentant. "I peeked."

She'd done it for him. She pretended to be miffed anyway. "A shocking violation of privacy."

"You wanted me to find it." He paused. "I'm not sure if you meant for anyone to notice the figures' similarity."

She shrugged. "I can't draw people. Not from life or my imagination. I copied a random lady from a fashion plate over and over again until I had the lines memorized, and now I use her for everything."

"As a substitution." His fingers touched one of her stray tendrils. "I can't help but notice the figure you chose looks remarkably like yourself."

"What?" She paused in the act of shoving it into her reticule, and opened the book instead.

Was it true? Had she managed to draw herself into fun, outlandish situations that would never happen to someone like her after all?

She flipped through the pages. He wasn't wrong. The ale-swilling, cheroot-smoking figure copied on every page shared every one of her physical characteristics.

"How did I not notice?"

"You noticed," he pointed out. "You just didn't notice that you noticed."

"And that eloquence is what makes you the greatest orator the House of Lords has ever known," she muttered.

"I'm not teasing you." He touched a knuckle to her chin. "I like your sketches. I wished you'd drawn me into the last one."

It was his new billiard room, looking exactly as it did now, with two exceptions. In the illustration, a magnificent John Thurston billiard table dominated the center of the room. And the lady figure—oh, very well, let's call her "Carole"—stood to one side with a billiard cue in her hand.

Alone.

"I wanted to draw you next to me," she admitted. "I just didn't know how."

"I'll help." He plucked the sketchbook from her fingers and took it over to his special shelf. As he drew directly on the page with a pencil, he kept his back to her—then turned around to present his modification with a flourish. "Voila!"

A giggle burst from her throat. Azureford's illustrative ability was on par with the Skeffington twins' chalk drawings on the street outside. He'd drawn a circle with a smiling face and a top hat. The boxy torso and equally boxy limbs were completely out of

112

proportion, but a billiard cue protruded from one rectangular hand. Instead of a lonely girl with no one to play with, the room now contained two friends likely to fill their evening with teasing and laughter.

"You can redo it when you figure out how to draw people," Azureford whispered.

She closed the book and pressed it to her heart. "It's perfect."

He grinned back at her impishly, looking perfectly kissable.

Carole fumbled the sketchbook back into her reticule, more to break her gaze from his than out of concern for her drawings.

"Now all we need is a billiard table, and you'll be on your way to winning hearts all over the land," she said lightly.

His muscles twitched.

She frowned. "What's wrong? Isn't that your plan?"

"It's the final step of a plan that's missing all the middle steps." He held up his fingers to count them out. "Step one, billiard table. Step three, marriage."

"That's not true," she reminded him. "You said this village—and this party—was your practice ground. If you can make friends with the people who don't matter, you'll have the confidence to flirt with the ladies who do."

He stared at her for a long moment. "I sounded like a prig."

"You sound like a lord," she corrected. "Not just any lord—a duke. We all know what that means. Your future bride is limited to the upper thousand. The rest of us choose from everybody else. It's not your fault. It's how the beau monde *is*."

"It gets worse." He sighed. "Both the bachelors and the hopeful brides are meant to accept the most selfish, coldblooded offer available. Who has the best blood? The highest connections? The oldest title? The most land? The biggest dowry? It's not marriage. It's expanding one's empire."

Each word made her feel emptier inside. "Is that what you're going to do?"

"It's what my parents did." He scrubbed his face with his hands. "It's what is expected of me. My sacred duty. A duke's responsibility to the title."

"I'll assume that means 'yes.'" She swallowed hard. He was looking for the perfect woman... who was her exact opposite. Her fingers went cold. If she'd been looking for proof that they were wrong for each other in every way, well, there it was. She'd *known* they could never be more than friends. The least she could do was act like one. "I'll help."

His gaze jerked up in surprise. "You'll help? How?"

"We'll playact until it becomes second nature. You be the Duke of Azureford, and I'll be... Debbie Debutante." Carole fanned her face with an invisible fan and affected a nasal voice and bored expression. "Ugh, if I have to dance with one more viscount or earl, when everyone knows my dowry is fit for a duchy... Why, good evening, Your Grace. I'm sure you know your very large estate abuts my even larger one. My mother is cousin to the king. Is that a waltz I hear?"

"Stop it." He knocked her pretend fan out of her hands. "That's more or less the conversation that led to my parents' union."

"How did that work out?"

"It didn't." His dark gaze was distant and angry. "Everything they wanted from each other they got with the wedding contract. Other than the night they conceived me, I'm not certain they were ever in the same room again." His eyes snapped to hers. "That is not the marriage I want."

She tilted her head. "What do you want?"

"To comply with my ducal duties with a woman I *like*." His expression was beseeching. "Wouldn't you?"

"I have no ducal duties and I'm never getting married," she replied evenly. "But we're not talking about me. Let's get you sorted first. How are you currently searching for a bride?"

"I visit Almack's." He gave a self-deprecating scoff. "And then stand there like a marble column."

She winced. "That might be the problem."

"I'll probably do the same thing at the party." He glared over her shoulder at the empty space in the middle of the room. "No matter how fancy my billiard table might be."

"All right." Carole rolled back her shoulders. She could do this. *They* could do this. "Let's make a plan. Bride-hunting can't be harder than the Excise Officers Allowance Act of 1812."

His eyes widened comically. "You were listening to me?"

She nodded. "Now listen to me. This is what we'll do. When the table arrives, I'll teach you how to play billiards... and in the meantime, I'll show you how to flirt with the ladies."

"In return," he said slowly, his expressive eyes not leaving hers, "I will do the same for you."

She blinked. "I already know how to play billiards."

"But do you have much experience with men?" The expression in his dark eyes was stormy. As though he would fulfill his ducal duties as required, even if part of him desired a woman who could never be a duchess.

A woman like… Carole.

"I'm not looking for a husband," she said carefully.

"Who said anything about marriage?" His brown eyes were serious. "Just because I must select a Society wife doesn't mean you have to give up your freedom."

"Ha." She pulled a face. If only that was a luxury she possessed. "Freedom to what?"

"To enjoy yourself." He stepped closer. "Like you said, I'm limited to future duchesses. You can do as you please."

Her throat went dry. Perhaps he, too, despised the thought of her promising herself to someone else. Perhaps he, too, wished they could ignore their divergent futures, just for a moment. Even if it could never be more than make-believe.

She licked her lips. "What would you do if you could do anything you wished?"

His gaze fell to her parted lips. "Do you want me to tell you or show you?"

"Show me." Her heart pounded defiantly but she didn't glance away.

Satisfaction glinted in his eyes. "With pleasure."

Then his hands cupped her cheeks and his lips covered hers.

Marble column? He was big and hard and strong, but there the comparison ended. His lips were warm on hers, gentle but firm. His thumb stroked her cheek so lightly she doubted he even realized he was doing so. Yet every caress sent flutters of desire through her belly.

When she opened her mouth to tell him so, to confess she was one mere kiss away from throwing all caution to the wind, his tongue swept inside to claim her. An electrifying bolt of desire shot through her. She felt every nudge, every lick, throughout her entire body.

She pressed herself against him to muffle the arousal tickling her skin, but the opposite occurred. With her bosom against his chest and his hands deep in her hair, their kiss was no longer tentative but a tidal wave of emotion that had just been waiting to be released.

All the times she'd glanced over at him beneath her eyelashes and wondered what it would be like to taste him? She was tasting him now. Gorging herself on his kisses. All the times his hand had brushed hers, all the brief "accidental" touches, all the times he had almost kissed her but held himself back? He wasn't holding back now. He was taking, demanding, giving, pleading. Two souls caught in a tug-of-war between *we shouldn't be doing this* and *I never want to stop.*

When she gasped for breath, his thumb stroked her cheek.

"Do you want me to stop?" His lips brushed hers.

She wrapped her hands about his neck. "Aren't you supposed to disregard what I want, shove me against the closest wall, and have your wicked way?"

He nibbled her lip. "Why would that work? No one wants to slam into a wall."

"You're the one who reads gothic novels," she reminded him between kisses. "Why would exposing my bosom by ripping open my bodice ever work? Stays are lined with whalebone."

"Are you saying I wouldn't win a fight against a whale?" He ran his hands down her back and splayed his fingers against her ribs.

She wished his fingers would keep exploring. "I'm saying no one has ever won a fight with a corset."

"Then you should definitely stop wearing them." He picked her up and swung her over to the sofa, tumbling backward so that she was the one on top. The one in control of whatever happened next.

She ran the pad of her thumb across the

very beginnings of stubble along the edge of his jaw. "Azureford?"

"Adam," he corrected, and touched her nose with his. "And you are?"

"Carole."

"Pleased to meet you."

He kissed her so well and for so long that she almost forgot what she'd been going to say.

"Were you going to ask me something?" he murmured.

"I was going to tell you something." She pushed up on his chest in order to meet his eyes, and did her best to muster up a good glare. "You led me to believe you were *bad* at this."

He grinned and kissed her again. "I'm enjoying this, too. It's different with you. I can be me and you can be you and none of it matters, since no one has to know."

For another woman, that last bit might have hit like a bucket of water. But the truth was, Carole had been thinking the same things. She had told him the truth. She *wasn't* going to marry. He had been equally honest. He needed a bride and it couldn't be her.

In the meantime, whatever happened between them, stayed between them. Resigning herself to the life of a spinster did not mean she had to turn down moments like these.

Until he left for good, this room would be their playground.

Just as she was dipping her head for another kiss, she caught sight of the clock out of the corner of her eye. She sprang up as if galvanized.

"Damn and blast." She shoved a fallen chunk of hair back into her bun and tried to shake the wrinkles from her skirt. At Adam's startled expression, she explained, "My father exits his study one time a week, and that time is... approximately five minutes ago. I have to go."

Without waiting for a response, she grabbed her reticule and dashed out the door.

"*Blast blast blast,*" she cursed as she raced toward her cottage.

There was no telling what might happen if Father walked into the billiard room and she wasn't there. He wasn't the sort to go looking for her. He might assume she was no longer interested and cease coming down from his study altogether. She would never see him again.

She skidded through the corridor, dodging questions from the housekeeper and the chambermaid and the—devil take it, why did everyone pick *right now* to become inexplicably incompetent at their jobs?

When she burst into the billiard room at last, her father was just chalking his cue.

She nearly collapsed in a puddle in relief.

"Father." She took a deep breath. "I think you should know—"

"The le Ducs will be here at any moment," he interrupted. "The butler forgot to iron the baize. Can you take care of it?"

She swallowed hard. "Yes, Father. Of course."

So much for having a private father-daughter tete-a-tete. That had been a once-in-a-lifetime opportunity. Now she had work to do. The butler hadn't ironed the baize because Carole hadn't been here to tell him to. That was her responsibility. Everything in this household was. She sighed in resignation. This cottage would fall down around them if she wasn't there to keep it propped up.

She could never leave.

*a*s much as he might have wished to, Adam did not greet Carole at the door with a kiss. He waited the full ten seconds for her maid to disappear with his butler, and *then* swung her into his arms.

She kissed him back not as if they'd just seen each other yesterday, but as though the two weeks that remained should only be spent in each other's arms.

He could not agree more.

When at last their lips parted, her hazel eyes gazed up at him from beneath her lashes. "I'm sorry I had to run off to meet my father."

"Don't be," Adam said, and meant it. Last night, he'd already added

> *Thoughtful*
> *Puts family first*

to his list of required qualities in a future bride.

"Besides," he added, "it gave me extra time to refine my flirting techniques."

She lifted a brow. "It's been one night, and already your technique is 'refined?'"

He nodded. "I made a chart."

"A chart of what?" she asked suspiciously.

"Opening lines." He affected an innocent expression. "I'll be the Duke of Azureford, you be Deborah Debutante. Ready?" He made an exquisite bow, then lowered his voice dramatically. "Why, Miss Deborah, your hand looks so heavy... Shall I hold it for you?"

Carole burst out laughing. "Do *not* incorporate that into your introductions."

"Brr." He hugged himself and gave an exaggerated shudder. "I must be a Christmas snowflake, because I've fallen for you."

She covered her face with her hands. "No. Absolutely not."

He pulled her hands from her face and gazed down at her soulfully. "May I borrow an atlas? I keep getting lost in your eyes."

"If she has an atlas, she'll hit you with it," Carole said warningly.

He stroked his chin as if in deep thought.

"Kiss me if I'm wrong, but... we're betrothed, right?"

She was laughing too hard to kiss him, but she tried to anyway. "You'll never be betrothed. You'll lose your Almack's voucher if the patronesses hear you. You're going to be the first duke spinster."

He pretended to be offended. "If you don't want my kisses, just return them!"

She swatted his shoulder, then stepped past him toward the dining room. "When will Thurston's crew arrive?"

Adam started to follow, then froze in place. Her long blond hair had been plaited to loop about her head in five golden rings. Because naturally it had. At this point, he was surprised she didn't arrive with five gold rings on each finger.

Carole glanced over her shoulder as if she'd sensed him paused to stare. "Is it the hair? I told Judith it was too much. She loves braiding the way some women love chocolate."

"Or pear tarts," he added wisely.

"You're right." She tapped the side of her chin. "If a blizzard blew through the village and I could only rescue one thing from this cottage... it would have to be your chef."

He clutched his chest. "You wound me! I am wounded!"

"Wait until your billiard table arrives," she said with a wicked smile. "Then you'll witness true destruction."

Little did she know the devastation had already begun. Spending the past few weeks with her had cracked a hole in who he thought he was, and what he believed himself capable of. He'd just been *bantering*, for God's sake. With her, he forgot to be shy.

"Adam!" she squealed as they entered the billiard room. "The table is here!"

He grinned at her. "Merry Christmas."

She threw herself in his arms. He swung her in a circle as he kissed her. They both knew it wasn't her table. They both also knew he wouldn't even be here for most of the year to enjoy it. And yet its shining presence in his cottage made him feel like they'd fought a battle side-by-side and emerged victorious.

He deposited her next to the cabinet and handed her a mace. "Here. Turn me into a genius."

"First lesson, genius..." She returned the mace to the cabinet and withdrew a cue instead. "Don't assume all women only play with the mace."

The back of his neck heated. "Duly noted."

"Additionally note that if you invite a woman to play and she does choose a mace, you must do the same. Both weapons must match."

He frowned. "Which is better?"

"That depends on the player. A billiards mace is a blunt object. Easy to wield, hard to control. Cues afford much greater precision— if one knows how to use them." Her eyes shone with mischievousness. "A woman might choose the mace as a tactical advantage. The gentleman is unlikely to have practiced with one, making him clumsy and inaccurate. If she had practiced, she'll win."

Adam stared at the cues and maces in his cabinet. They hadn't even started playing yet and already the first decision appeared to be between two items that were simultaneously better and worse than each other.

"Owning a billiard room will be no help if all you're going to do is stand about glaring at your equipment." She handed him a cue. "Some men 'chalk' the leather tip by smashing it overhead against the plaster. We are not barbarians. We use chalk."

He accepted a piece and copied her movements.

"Don't chalk over the baize. Dust will get everywhere. Don't knock your cue against the table for the same reason." She ran her fingers lightly over the edge of the billiard table, then grinned up at him. "I can scarcely credit that

I'll be the first person to play on this table. It feels like history being made."

"It is history," he assured her. "It's the first time you're playing on this table, and the first time I'm playing on *any* table. We should commission a plaque. Or some kind of statue."

"I drew you a sketch. That's good enough. We can talk about trophies when you start scoring points." She arranged the two ivory balls and single red ball on the table. "Watch. It works like this."

For the next hour, she patiently showed him basic shot after basic shot, repeating the same movements dozens of times and then demanding the same from him.

It might have been easier to concentrate on the instructions if she hadn't placed her hands just below his waistband to arrange his stance, or settled her hands over his to guide his shot. With Carole's soft, curvy body brushing against his at every turn, Adam had about as much chance of flying to the moon as managing to hit the right cue ball.

Between shots, he tried to conceal his fractured concentration by jotting notes in a special journal he'd purchased just for this reason, but capturing a motion in words proved impossible. Once she realized what he was about, she took pity on him—and took control of the journal. After explaining each shot, she'd sketch the table in his book, complete with all three balls, the correct position of the cue, and little arcing arrows with notations as to the proper angles for each shot.

Adam nodded sagely and tried to pretend he could feel the difference between a twenty-degree angle and a thirty-degree angle, but mostly he was doing his best just to hit the ball he was aiming for.

"My cue ball has a black dot," she explained. "Yours does not. If this was an actual game, we would score 'cannons' by knocking our cue ball into the red ball and the other ball, in any order."

He frowned. "They don't have to go into the pockets?"

"Not for a cannon. You're thinking of hazards." She demonstrated. "A 'winning hazard' means potting the red ball by striking it with your cue ball. That shot is worth slightly more than using your cue ball to pot your opponent's."

"How much more?"

"That depends." She shrugged. "There is no official rulebook. Players agree on points and rules before they begin. In my experience, potting the opponent's cue and making a cannon are each worth two points. Potting the red ball is three. Fouls subtract two in my family, but many players add two to the opponent's score instead. And then there are 'losing hazards.'"

"How many points do 'losing hazards' take away?"

"None. Striking your cue into your opponent's so that you pot your own ball is two points. Doing it to the red one is three. You keep going until there are no balls or you make a foul, such as hitting no balls at all or making more than fifteen hazards in a row. Understand?"

He stared at the table in bafflement. "Clear as crystal."

She burst out laughing. "Don't worry. I remember what it felt like not to understand how anything worked. Back then, I could barely lift my own cue." She gave him a crooked grin. "You can do this. Put down the journal. Take a shot."

"At the House of Lords, I feel invincible and all-knowing," he grumbled as he lined up what he hoped was a cannon. "Essentially the opposite of how I feel at this moment."

"Proficiency comes with practice," she said as she returned the balls to their original position and motioned for him to start again. "I doubt you were the Dukest of All Dukes your very first day in Parliament."

"You weren't there," he answered with fake hauteur. "I was legendary."

"You are *now*," she agreed, peering up at him sideways from her cue stick. "So am I."

She proceeded to jump her cue ball over the top of the red ball in order to pocket Adam's.

"How did you…" He floundered wordlessly. "Shouldn't witchcraft be a foul?"

"Go and make a law against magic," she teased, and sashayed around the table to take her next shot.

CHAPTER 11

*C*arole did her best to keep her posture perfect as Judith fashioned her hair into a series of interlocking twists.

It wasn't that she was impatient—although, yes, sometimes she was that. But today she was keeping extra still because Judith had insisted on a complicated hair arrangement, despite spending the first hour of the morning surreptitiously trying to loosen her gnarled fingers.

An uneasy sensation twisted in Carole's belly. She now suspected that Judith's recent preoccupation with pins and curling tongs wasn't because of some feminine standard for lady billiard instructors, but because Judith feared there would not be many more years in which her arthritic fingers could plait hair at all.

Carole gazed in the looking-glass at her

maid's beloved lined face. Hair didn't matter. Who cared if a spinster's locks closely resembled a rat's nest? Judith was irreplaceable. The closest thing to a mother Carole had experienced in fifteen long years. Judith deserved to grow old any deuced way she pleased. Even if that meant curling tongs every morning and stolen moments with the neighbor's butler every afternoon.

When Azureford had returned to London last autumn, Swinton had stayed behind. When the party had passed and Azureford once again left their village behind, Judith at least would not be brokenhearted. Carole would coax her father to reduce Judith's working hours, so that she had more time to live her life.

As for Carole… what did her heart have to do with anything? She'd be too busy running the household and taking care of her father to have time to even daydream about anyone else.

She hoped.

"Parcel for you, miss." Rhoda popped into the room to set a brown-paper parcel on the dressing table.

"I'd wager that's the geometry tome you've been waiting for." Judith wrinkled her nose and grimaced. "Don't know how anyone can be more excited about dry old numbers and lines than the pretty fashion plates in La Belle Assemblée."

Carole eyed the crisp brown rectangle. She'd wager Judith was right. That was definitely the book she'd been dying to possess all year. Yet its charms paled against the pleasures awaiting her next door. Reading could wait. There would be plenty of time for Pythagoras once Adam was gone.

"There." Judith fluffed Carole's sleeves. "If he hasn't stolen a kiss by now, he will today."

Carole's cheeks flushed bright red.

"Oh?" Judith wiggled her silver eyebrows, blue eyes crinkling with mischief. "Excellent work."

"I suppose you've been 'working' with Swinton?" Carole asked archly.

"Eh? What's that? These ears aren't what they used to be." But a pretty flush covered Judith's face, too. "Come along, come along. Haven't you a billiard lesson to teach?"

Grinning, they raced from the bedchamber to the front door.

Mrs. MacDonald stood there waiting, a scrap of paper in her hand. "Miss Quincy, the menu—"

—was always the same, with only minor variations due to the changing seasons. After her mother died, Carole had taken over the role of approving each day's course, but she'd never had cause to tell the housekeeper *no*. Whatever was on that paper was perfectly fine. And if it wasn't, Father was unlikely to notice anyway.

"Whatever you suggest, Mrs. MacDonald." Carole gave an encouraging smile. "You know the kitchen as well as I do. I trust your judgment."

And she was in a hurry. Judith was right. There was a billiard lesson to teach.

"Thank you, miss," the housekeeper stammered in wonderment, and stepped away from the door.

Carole and Judith flew next door to the Duke of Azureford's summer cottage. Swinton opened the door wide before they were halfway up the front path. Adam stood right beside his butler, neither bothering to hide that they'd been awaiting the ladies' arrival with just as much anticipation.

"I ought to…" Swinton began, and cleared his throat.

"I can help," Judith said quickly.

Carole and Adam were already almost at the billiard room and missed the rest of whatever fictional explanation they were making up on the spot.

He stole a kiss the moment they were out of sight.

Every moment in his arms was like spring

after a long winter. A riot of color, of scent, of taste. Everything seemed to bloom at once, filling her with a desire so sharp and so sweet she thought she might swoon from the headiness.

When she regained her breath, Carole shook her finger. "That's the last of the free kisses, Your Grace. If you want more, you'll have to earn them."

"Can I earn them with the extremely clever opening lines I've been practicing?" He asked innocently.

She selected a cue. "You'd better hope you've been practicing billiards. Any other questions?"

His eyes twinkled. "If I were to ask you for one more kiss, would your answer be the same as the answer to this question?"

"Beast." Laughing, she shoved a cue into his hands. "Show me a cannon."

"You have no idea how much I'd like to," he murmured.

Carole arranged the three balls on the baize. "You first. Three in a row earns a kiss."

"*Three* in a row?" His cockiness turned into dubiousness.

She took pity. "Can you do two in a row?"

"Yes," he said without hesitation. "Watch."

He chalked the leather tip of the cue, aligned himself at the far end of the table, then struck his ivory so that it hit Carole's first, and then the red ball.

She clapped her hands. "Do it again."

He strutted to the opposite side of the table, carefully arranged his cue, then hit first the red, and then Carole's ivory.

"Two in a row, as promised." She lifted her gaze from the table. "Now what?"

He pulled a face. "Now is when it falls apart. The second cannon takes a fair bit of luck, and a third is all but impossible. No one could hit a cannon with the balls all spread out like this."

"Exactly." She returned them to their original position and picked up her cue. "This is how you hit both balls and send them only as far as you want them to go."

Although he was inexperienced with billiards, Adam copied her motions with control and grace. Not only was he physically in fine form, his grace and coordination were impressive. He was more than a quick study. He was talented. It wouldn't be long at all before he no longer needed her.

Her stomach twisted with dread at the impending loss. She would have to try even harder to maintain emotional distance.

This flirtation is just a game, she reminded herself sternly. *You might not be thinking of anyone but him, but Adam is practicing in order to woo someone else.*

She could play along. She'd been playing games her entire life. It was all she had.

"Afternoon post, Your Grace." A footman entered the billiard room with a silver tray, and headed straight toward Adam.

"Leave it on the table, please," Adam responded without looking up from the shot he was aligning.

The footman started with obvious surprise, then did as requested. He sent one last intrigued look over his shoulder before disappearing back into the corridor.

Carole watched with interest. It was obvious the footman had fully expected Adam to immediately drop whatever he was doing to attend to his correspondence. Either Adam regularly received letters of utmost importance... or he was breaking a long-held habit simply because he preferred to spend his time with Carole. Although her stomach fluttered, she tried not to read too much into it.

She cleared her throat. "If you need to pause our lesson to review your correspondence..."

He glanced up, brown eyes wide and a little confused, as if he'd already forgotten the footman's interruption.

"I already know what it is." He shrugged a shoulder. "A few different committees want to nominate me as leader, but I barely have enough time to dedicate to them all as it is. They're trying to convince me otherwise."

She arranged the balls in a new configuration. "Are their causes worthy?"

"Very." He frowned at the new lineup. "What am I supposed to do with that?"

"When the red ball and your ivory are equidistant from the side, aim to hit here—" She touched a point exactly between them. "—and your cue ball will hit its mark."

"Maybe," he muttered, but did as she suggested.

His ivory barely whiffed the red ball, lacking enough force to properly pot it, but making the promised contact all the same. Adam's eyes lit with surprise and triumph. "Can you add it to the journal?"

"With pleasure."

While he realigned the balls to try again, she sketched several similar shots into his journal, careful to annotate each with angles and degrees. He might tease her about the geometry, but Adam was as analytical as she was. Just as he did in the House of Lords, Adam would soon be able to look at a billiard table and see the whole picture, as well as how to change it.

Her pencil faltered. Thinking of the House of Lords only reminded her that soon he would be gone. London claimed him more than half of each year. And Parliament wasn't the only thing that called him. There were dinner soirées and cotillions and all the young ladies just waiting to be swept off their feet.

The hour spent painstakingly pinning and curling her hair now seemed trite and silly. She was not competing. She'd lost before she'd begun.

She closed the journal. "You're going to do very well at your party. Well, you won't beat the le Ducs, but nor will you embarrass yourself. That is, unless you use those horrid introductions."

"I hope they'll make me memorable and interesting. Right now, no one knows anything about me." His eyes met hers. "Except you."

"Which gives me the expertise to point out you're already interesting." Heaven knew, *she* could not cease thinking about him. "If you have to become something you're not to attract the right person, then she's not the right person."

"My parents prided themselves on not bending an inch for anyone else, not even each other, and all they gained from selfish stubbornness was misery." His eyes shuttered.

"They missed their chance. I vowed I wouldn't miss mine."

She nodded in empathy. Her parents *had* been happy. Blissfully so. The misery hadn't come until afterward. Her chest tightened with resolve. The best part of spinsterhood was never risking the pain of loss. "What will determine the right one?"

His jaw tightened. "To me, 'duchess material' means so much more than social connections and a vast dowry. Our personalities need to match, too. I don't want a marriage where each one 'wins' but 'loses.'"

Carole understood. She even agreed. So why did it feel like she was the one who would lose?

CHAPTER 12

*A*dam could not wait to show Carole how he'd mastered her latest challenge.

When she'd first started spouting algebraic formulas such as, "If your ivory is three times as far from the rail as the red ball, aim for a point four-fifths of the distance to the red one," he'd thought she'd lost her mind. It sounded like the sort of mathematics others had always hated: *If two mail coaches leave London with odd numbers of horses, and each horse can travel at a maximum speed of...*

But she was right. It had taken three long hours and two pots of tea to finally master, but he could now pot the red ball whenever its distance from the side was a calculable factor of his ivory's distance to—

Adam chuckled and lined up another shot. Now even his *thoughts* sounded like Carole. It was as though the sight of a billiard table conjured her to mind.

Or, really, the sight of anything. Or nothing. Even when lying in bed with his eyes closed, she was still all he could think about. Which was good, because it meant there was no space left in his brain to think about how it would feel when she was no longer about.

As eager as he was to impress her with his latest billiard trick, she walked through the door looking so frazzled that he set down his cue and immediately rang for tea.

He lifted her hands in his. "What's wrong?"

"Nothing." She wrapped her arms about herself and shuddered. "My father."

Dread encased Adam's stomach as he reached for her. "Your father has fallen ill?"

"I don't think so. Not physically. He suffers attacks of melancholy." She leaned her cheek against Adam's chest, her voice taut to the point of breaking. "Father spends all day shut away in his study, except when he can't even do that."

"Like today." Adam stroked her hair.

She nodded and burrowed closer. "Father will be himself again in a few days; or, at least, what's left of himself. But he's not truly living. He hasn't since my mother died."

"It's not your fault." Adam tried to think of

a solution. "Perhaps… perhaps what he needs is to meet someone new."

She pushed away from him. "Father *did* meet someone. The love of his life. There's one special person out there for each of us. He met her; he married her; she died."

"I know people find the notion of 'one' true love romantic, but to me it's just… sad."

"It's not emotion," she insisted. "It's maths. Every problem has a perfect solution."

"Does it?" he said doubtfully. "I rather think the perfect match is two *im*perfect people who happen to be perfect for each other. Since we're all imperfect, it's stands to reason that there are plenty of fish in the sea—"

"My mother was The One." Her fierce voice cracked, and a glassy sheen coated her eyes.

"Of course she was," he agreed quickly. "She was absolutely the perfect and only One *then*, but your father lives *now*. Finding happiness a second time doesn't cancel out the first time." He tried to find words she would understand. "Love is addition, not subtraction."

"It doesn't feel that way." With trembling hands, she slid a finger under her necklace and pulled a slender golden ring up from her bodice. "This was my mother's. I keep it next to my heart. It first belonged to her mother, and her mother's mother, and the grand-mother before that."

She dropped the necklace and the ring returned to its hiding spot.

"I'm breaking the chain," she said quietly. "On purpose. That's the only way to be certain I won't lose my daughter and my daughter won't lose me."

There was nothing he could say to take away her pain, so he pulled her into his arms and said nothing.

He understood why she believed life was a formula that could be learned. Why she *needed* to believe every problem had a solution. But by reaching for answers that might not exist, peace would forever evade her. He lay his cheek against her soft hair.

"It's all right to want things you can't have," he murmured. "It's all right not to be perfect; to be sad; to be happy. It makes you human, not incomplete."

She lifted her face from his cravat and gave a wobbly smile. "But is that enough?"

"It's more than enough," he said softly. "*You're* enough. Plenty of the fish in the sea are very bitter that you're not out there swimming with them."

She snorted. "*Do* fish get bitter?"

Adam was starting to think maybe they did.

He was a fish. *He* was in the sea. No—she was in the sea and he was in a private aquarium with a view of the water. His glass palace was expensive and protected, up high on a pedestal, boxed in on every side. Her boundaries were as limitless as the ocean. She could swim as far away as she wanted, but she was right here in his arms.

Marrying her would be the opposite of fitting in. Instead of talking *to* him, the peers he was trying so hard to fit in with were more likely to talk *about* him. Not to mention his duty to the title. And yet...

He didn't need a fortuneteller to see his future: his bride would be the wealthy daughter of a fellow peer. Well-connected, well dressed, and well bred, with a flawless reputation and a dowry whose property rivaled his own. In all his thirty years, he'd never questioned the strictures he was meant to follow and the ideals he was meant to live up to. Now he was wondering whether that path was the right path.

What if he *didn't* marry a High Society debutante? What if he took an unconventional bride? What was the worst that could happen? And if the worst *did* happen... would it still be worth it?

He cleared his throat. "Carole?"

Her hazel eyes peered up at him from beneath her lashes. "Yes?"

He tucked a tendril of golden hair behind her ear. "We're always here, in my billiard room. Out of the way. Secretive. What do you think of... Would it be all right for me to call on you tomorrow instead?"

Calling wasn't the same as proposing. All sorts of gentlemen paid twenty-minute afternoon visits to all sorts of ladies. Although, perhaps not typically dukes knocking at the cottage of—

He needn't have worried. Carole reared back as though he'd doused her in water.

"Please don't." She pulled an expression that might have been comical, had it not twisted a knife in his chest. "If you come to our door, my father would think it *meant* something."

Which told him everything he needed to know.

"Of course," he murmured. "It's better like this."

Just like billiards, the rules were clear. When the game was over, it was over.

Effectively being rebuffed before he could progress far enough to ask a question ought to have turned him against the idea altogether. Instead, his respect for her only grew. Carole had never left him unclear as to where things stood. As far as she was concerned, she wasn't missing a man. As far as Adam was concerned, that was absolutely true. Carole was marvelous in her own right.

But it did let him know that he needed to add

even though she doesn't need me... still wants me.

to his list of requirements.

CHAPTER 13

*C*arole hunched over her writing table, filling the last page in her sketchbook with yet another illustration of a fantasy life starring her and Adam. Her skill with portraying real-life people had not improved, but it took little effort to copy Adam's simple, top-hat-wearing rectangle-man into the drawings.

The ridiculous tableau of Fashion Plate Lady and Rectangle Man somehow made her fantastical settings seem all the more real. As though it really was the two of them riding horses through the evergreens, waltzing in the castle ballroom, curled up next to each other before a winter fire.

Truth was, in just a few days, they would be nothing at all. His party was the following night. Whether tomorrow went well or badly did not signify. He had promised to stay for a month and it had already been five weeks. She was taking more than her share. Soon, it would be time to let go.

But not until after tonight.

She shoved the sketchbook back into her reticule and turned to face the looking-glass. Judith had wanted to save the prettiest gown for the night of the party. Carole didn't want to wait to look her best until Adam's gaze was on other women. Tonight was the last night she would have him all to herself.

Judith had draped her in her finest gown: an underdress of deep blue covered with white gauze, complete with matching puffed sleeves and French-heeled slippers. This was as close as Carole had ever come to matching the elegant illustrations in her fashion plates. Not even a hair was out of place.

With a final pinch of her cheeks to give them color, she swept out of her cottage and over to his.

His eyes widened when she walked through the door.

Not because she had vastly overdressed for an ordinary occasion. But because he'd done the same thing, too.

His snowy white cravat contrasted sharply with the black superfine coat molded to his body. His formal black breeches and emerald green silk waistcoat looked fit for a ballroom.

Even his Hessians were probably champagne shined. Her heart gave a little flutter.

He gave a self-deprecating grin at her expression. "One's last night feels like a momentous occasion."

She matched his smile. It wasn't his last night in Cressmouth. It was their last night alone together. Tomorrow night was the party. His opportunity to win the hearts of every other female in town. To practice for when it really mattered. A flash of jealousy stabbed through her. She tried fruitlessly to push it away. Watching him flirt with someone else was going to kill her. Watching him drive away to marry someone else…

Tomorrow, she reminded herself. There was still tonight. They could make this evening anything they pleased. Celebrate however they wished. She rose to her toes, laced her hands about his neck, and kissed him.

This was not a kiss of innocence or experimentation. She knew his mouth as well as her own. Loved the firmness of his lips, the heat of his tongue. Not for the first time, she wondered how his kisses would feel against the rest of her body. Desire unfurled at the familiar fantasy. Hours remained before they had to say goodbye.

"One more game?" she suggested. "Winner

takes all."

His dark eyes didn't leave hers. "All of what?"

"Anything he wants," she said softly.

He kissed her again. "I'll get the cues."

Instead of following him to the table, she wandered over to his reading nook. When and if Adam returned to Cressmouth, his father's favorite books would be here waiting. Battered spines, torn pages, and all.

She pulled her sketchbook from her reticule and hesitated. This wasn't a mere "favorite" possession. This was a piece of her soul. Fitting, she supposed.

Before she could change her mind, she opened the book to the first sketch of Fashion Plate Lady and Rectangle Man smiling and laughing in Adam's billiard room. Her heart thumped. Quickly, she dogeared the page, bent the spine, and then shoved the volume onto the shelf where it wouldn't be noticed for a long while.

If Adam never returned to Cressmouth, he would take this collection with him... and whenever he missed what they used to have, all he would have to do was take this book from its shelf, run his finger along the creases her hands had made, and lose himself in the eternal adventures of a world that never was, knowing she had done the very same.

She shoved her empty reticule into a hidden skirt pocket just as he finished arranging the table.

He gestured toward the beautiful table she'd once believed the finest thing on earth. "Ivory ball or black dot, madam? Lady's choice."

Carole didn't give a damn about billiards. She wanted Adam.

Just this once.

"If I surrendered…" She gazed up at him and licked her lips. "What would you take?"

"Everything," he answered without hesitation. "You made the rules."

She wrapped her arms about his neck. "Then I surrender."

His mouth met hers and there was no more conversation.

She gave herself over to sensation. His hands were warm and familiar against her curves, his tongue an iron to stoke the fire. These were flames that nothing could extinguish.

What would she do to have more than one night? Could she perhaps become his summer mistress? Would a few torrid weeks every year be enough? Or was one goodbye all she would ever be able to bear?

She shoved the thoughts of a bittersweet future away and concentrated on fully experiencing every moment, while she could still revel in his embrace. She loved the familiar hard planes of his muscles, the warmth of his strong arms, the equally breathless passion in every kiss.

"Winner takes all?" he murmured against the base of her throat.

"Absolutely everything," she confirmed, her raspy voice laden with desire.

He slid his hands to cup her bottom and lifted her hips to straddle his.

It took a second for her to realize he meant to position her on the edge of the rail.

"Watch the table," she gasped between kisses.

"If we break it, I'll buy another one," he growled as he nuzzled the top of her bosom.

She arched her spine to give him better access. "But the baize—"

"Swinton knows how to iron."

"*John Thurston* made this. If it tears, the billiard gods will curse you."

He lifted his head. "Are there sofa gods?"

"Sofa gods love wrinkles," she assured him.

"Hallelujah." He swung her toward the satin-covered cushions. "Let's go and create some wrinkles."

Her arms reached for him as she tumbled backward onto the sofa. She could not withstand even a hairsbreadth of space between them. He was too dangerous to let go. Too ephemeral. He made her question things she'd previously accepted as fact. Like not wanting a partner in life. Like not needing love.

Good God, she was in *love*? Carole's throat went dry in horror.

Her kisses were so urgent because she could not stand the thought of him marrying someone else. And yet she would not beg him to stay. He couldn't do so if he wanted to. The dukedom came first. He was as tied to London as she was to Cressmouth. She had her household. He had the House of Lords. What they couldn't have was each other.

Except for right now. Right here. Tonight.

She kissed him with everything she'd been holding back; every fear, every surreptitious glance, every long night of endless longing, every heartbeat that called his name. She might not have him forever, but she would absolutely have him tonight.

He yanked up the hem of her skirt and slid his hand slowly, deliciously, toward the junction of her thighs. Her inner muscles tightened deliciously in anticipation. She let her legs fall wide to give him greater access. Already her core pulsed with need as if it ached for the stroke of his fingers. He paused inches from where she wanted his touch most.

"Carole." He lifted his lips from hers to meet her eyes. "What exactly are we doing?"

She wriggled her hips to try and get closer to his hand. "I believe it's called love-making?"

"Have you done this before?"

"Does it matter?"

He removed his hand. "I'm not going to ruin you."

"You can't ruin me. *I'm* having my way with *you*." She dug her fingers into a satin pillow in frustration. "I willingly relinquish my virginity. It doesn't matter. I'm not going to marry anyway."

"*You* matter." He brushed the pad of his thumb against her cheek. "I like you too much to want our bodies to make promises they're not going to keep."

"I don't mind," she tried again, but he was already ending their embrace and pulling her to her feet.

He kissed her long and hard, as though for the final time. Perhaps it was. When he stepped back out of reach, her chest already felt empty inside. It did not help that his eyes looked just as miserable.

"I'll think of you tonight and every night." His voice was gruff. He did not reach for her again. "It will have to be enough."

It wouldn't be, of course. But they could pretend.

CHAPTER 14

*I*t was an unmitigated crush. Adam could barely shift his weight without brushing shoulders with three different people. For a village with approximately a thousand inhabitants, it felt like most of the population was stuffed inside his summer cottage.

Despite this, Adam had not expected Carole to make an appearance. The previous encounter had ended abruptly, with both of them at odds with the other. She seemed to think sharing one night together would somehow be sufficient. He was already going to have enough trouble forgetting her, without adding *making love on the sofa* to the list of things forever marked with her presence.

A cluster of locals sat at the table that he and Carole had used to plan the renovation. A group of ladies sipped from the china he and Carole had used to take tea. A handful of neighbors crowded the enclave where Carole had created his reading nook. A dozen others surrounded the billiard room where he and Carole had spent the past fortnight, practically inseparable.

Now she was introducing him to so many people, he could barely keep his own name straight.

"Olive, may I present the Duke of Azureford? Your Grace, this is Miss Harper. She's phenomenal with horses."

"Nick and Penelope, may I present the Duke of Azureford? Your Grace, this is Mr. and Mrs. Pringle. She's the best perfumer in England, and he's an incorrigible rogue."

"Angelica, may I present the Duke of Azureford? Your Grace, this is Miss Parker, an extremely talented jeweler."

"Désirée, may I present the Duke of Azureford? Your Grace, this is Mademoiselle le Duc. She taught me how to curse in French."

"Chris and Gloria, may I present the Duke of Azureford? Your Grace, this is Mr. and Mrs. Pringle."

Wait—hadn't there *already* been a Mr. and Mrs. Pringle? Adam's head started to pound. Nonetheless, he smiled and nodded and bowed and murmured what he hoped would pass as charming manners, given the roar of surrounding conversation drowned out his words.

Carole was taking extra care not only to provide him with helpful tidbits to remember each person by, but also ensure every local unwed young lady had her turn to be presented to Adam. Regardless of how the previous evening had deteriorated, Carole was doing an admirable job of upholding her side of what was becoming an increasingly unwanted bargain. The more she nudged nubile young ladies into his path, the more he only wanted to spend all his time with *her.*

He wasn't alone in his feelings. The greatest obstacle to Carole introducing him to every woman in sight was that everyone in the village elbowed and jostled in order to spend as much time as possible with Carole.

Apparently, she'd saved a theatre director from something or other, was on a first-name basis with the castle solicitor and all of her neighbors, had helped the Duke of Nottingvale prepare for his annual Christmastide house party…

Carole wasn't just *from* this village. She was its heartbeat.

"Miss Shelling is a journalist," she was

saying now. "Eve, tell His Grace about your work with the Cressmouth Gazette."

Adam tried to listen, truly he did, but it was difficult to pay attention to anyone else when Carole was standing right in front of him. He adored how friendly she was, how happy she made others feel, how effortless she made it look. How at home she was, right here atop a tiny mountain in the northernmost corner of England.

Despite his title and wealth, Carole seemed on an even higher rung. Unobtainable. Unreachable. Perhaps because she didn't give a damn about his money and his title. The fact that Adam was a duke was actually a strike against him. He was needed elsewhere and she was needed here. That's why he was supposed to be practicing his conversational parries and flirtation methods for his prodigal return as New Adam.

Yet it was getting harder and harder to work up enthusiasm to "graduate" from Cressmouth to London. Now that he knew what it was like to spend five weeks of relaxed, enjoyable, passionate, silly, delightful days with someone, he didn't want to go back to... *not*.

When Carole was pulled away by yet another admirer, Swinton somehow managed to sidle up to Adam. "Enjoying your farewell party, Your Grace?"

Swinton already knew the answer. He'd been part of the household since before Adam was born. Life with his parents had always been complicated, but his relationship with Swinton had always been straightforward. He'd known everything about Adam from his first newborn cry to last night's extra glasses of wine, which Adam had deeply regretted this morning. As Swinton had said he would. He was butler, he was father figure, he was a thorn in Adam's side. And positively irreplaceable.

Adam sent him a sour look. "Shouldn't you be minding the door?"

"We can't fit anyone else." Swinton's expression was pleased. "Everyone is already inside."

"Fair enough."

Swinton glanced over his shoulder. "Miss Quincy is looking lovely tonight."

"She's always lovely," Adam answered automatically. He hadn't been able to take his eyes off her all night.

Her hazel eyes were especially bright tonight, her lips as kissable as ever. The edges of her sunlight-colored gown were decorated with tiny yellow rosebuds at the arms, hem, neck, and under-bodice, making five golden rings of—

"Ha," he told Swinton. "Very humorous."

Swinton looked back at him innocently.

Adam deeply regretted his drunken confession about the fortuneteller and following the signs. "She said I'd see *five* gold rings. Not one hundred and five. I'm far past that amount, which proves her wrong."

"Or it proves you're too stubborn to take a hint," Swinton said smugly, and melted back into the crowd before Adam could respond.

Was he missing his best chance at happiness? He hadn't wanted to reduce Carole to nothing but a temporary lover, but nor had he made her a better offer. Would he? *Could* he?

What would New Adam do?

New Adam wasn't shy and awkward but bold and confident. New Adam wouldn't waste time wooing the wrong women when the right one was there in his sights. When it came to choosing a wife, the only preferences that mattered would be his own. So what did he truly desire?

He didn't just want Carole to be happy. He wanted to be the one who made her happy. The one who stood at her side, no matter what. The one she loved, as much as he loved her.

Equal parts fear and panic twisted in his

stomach. His chest tightened until his galloping heart threatened to break free. His palms were clammy; his throat too dry to speak.

Being in love wasn't the end of the world, he promised himself. Neither was being shy. But he'd vowed not to hold back with her. Not after all this. He'd never forgive himself if he didn't seize the opportunity to be completely honest with her, come what may.

And they had a good thing, did they not? No—a *great* thing. A splendid thing. Spinsterhood was unnecessary. Marriage was a huge step, but worth the leap if they could take it together. Surely she'd see that.

Maybe she'd see that.

He squared his shoulders. Old Adam would not have tried to win the hand of the girl of his dreams because he knew he'd be too shy to succeed. New Adam would probably always be awkward at such things, but he was going to try anyway. There was no one else he'd rather spend the rest of his life with.

It was about time he let her know.

CHAPTER 15

*C*arole's cheeks ached from the effort of maintaining a happy expression. She hadn't stopped talking and smiling for hours. Introducing her favorite people in the world to Adam should have been a joyful occasion, but instead she felt like an automaton; performing exactly as she was programmed to. And it was her own blasted fault.

Adam hadn't sprung this party on her as a surprise. He'd been candid about his reasons for visiting the village she called home since the beginning. She'd volunteered to *help* him, for the love of crumpets. They both understood the game. *She* had been the one to try and change the rules with an intimate encounter on top of his sofa.

Him gently refusing to complicate something simple had been the right answer. The only answer.

Just look at this party. A roaring success! He wasn't standing in the corner glaring wordlessly at his guests, but mingling. Conversing. He'd even played half of a billiard game with Lucien le Duc before so many people crowded the room as to make wielding a cue impossible.

She'd liked Adam from the first, but now he was even better. More engaging, more magnetic. With or without deep pockets and a fancy title, when he returned to London for the Season, ladies would be lined up at Almack's to waltz with *him*.

At least she wouldn't be there to see it.

Carole turned back to the party. She could cope with this. She'd prepared for this. It was what they both wanted.

When at last the night had stretched so long that dawn was bleeding into the sky, most of the guests returned to their homes and only a few stragglers remained.

"Wait," Adam said softly, his warm lips brushing her ear. "I need to talk to you."

They had spent the past six hours repeating pleasantries and introductions until their voices went hoarse, but there had been no time to *talk*. She wasn't certain she wished to. Or that there were any words left in her throat at all.

Yet her feet stayed planted in the middle of

his drawing room as he and his butler master-fully shooed the rest of the flock out the door without them noticing they were being evicted.

Once again, she and Adam were alone.

It didn't feel like before. Perhaps nothing ever would.

"Carole," he began, his expression serious and stern.

She waited.

No further comment seemed forthcoming.

"It was a good party," she assured him, the words tumbling over each other like dead leaves. "You will be the toast of the ton next Season, I swear it. Gentlemen begging for billiard games, ladies swooning over each other left and right, vying for the chance to be your duchess—"

"You." He drew himself up, as tall and imposing as he must appear when he addressed his peers in the House of Lords. "I want to marry you."

She blinked. Apparently two could change the rules.

"No, you don't," she reminded him. They both knew it could not work. "You want a High Society debutante with good blood, advantageous connections, a large dowry, vast properties, and an Almack's voucher. I have none of those things."

"I know." His expression was tortured. "It doesn't matter. What we have is better."

He meant this, she realized in wonder. This was a real proposal. If she said yes, he would do it.

The exquisite crack in her heart made her realize she would do absolutely anything to keep him in her life… except ruin his.

She wasn't *haut ton*. He'd spent the evening being introduced to all the "connections" she had. There were no family estates in her dowry. The amount wouldn't even cover what he'd spent on new windows. There was no Almack's voucher. She'd never even been formally presented to Society.

Marrying her wouldn't be an advantage. It would be an albatross.

"Adam," she began, and then stopped. The truth was too hard to say.

The only reason he thought he wanted her was because he'd never had a connection like this with anyone else. It wasn't *Carole* who was special. It was the novelty of coming out of his shell.

When he returned to London, more secure and more confident, he would discover that any number of women would be delighted to be the object of his attention. Waltzes, promenades, even billiards. Carole wasn't unique. In a matter of weeks, he would find someone just like her who could also offer all the other characteristics that she could not.

With that woman, with the better choice, he would be able to achieve so much more. Not just enrich his duchy, but expand his connections, be more popular with the set in Parliament. The thought made her shake with panic and jealousy and bitterness. But for every problem, no matter how hard, there was always one right answer.

She kissed him on his cheek and whispered, "No."

The only solution was goodbye.

That was it. The last of the few belongings Adam cared to keep were loaded into his coach. Two hours past dawn, and his driver was already waiting for him beside the carriage.

Under other circumstance, Adam might've taken one last walk through the cottage, just to be certain he wasn't leaving anything important behind. But today he could not bear to look at the billiard room. He knew exactly what he was leaving behind.

Carole had said no.

He gripped the doorframe until his

knuckles went white. The idea of walking away from this cottage, walking away from *Carole*, made him dizzy. His heart was incomplete without her. Yet he would have to go to London alone. Have to marry someone else, knowing full well his heart was hundreds of miles north.

Perhaps Carole would wed someone else, too. She claimed she didn't want to, but maybe she just didn't want to marry *him*.

He could try to convince her, but her happiness came first—and, frankly, so did his. Having to *talk* an unwilling woman into marrying him was not the equal, loving union he'd been hoping for. If she didn't want him, then she wasn't the right one after all.

"Ready, Your Grace?" asked the driver.

It was then that Adam realized his proposal had lacked the most important words of all. He'd gotten the *Marry me* bit out, and forgotten the *I love you*. His stomach twisted. He covered his burning cheeks with his hand. Of all the henwitted mistakes a lovesick swain could make during a proposal...

Then again, she hadn't said she loved him, either. Or asked about feelings at all. Her answer was just... *no*.

He would have to respect her wishes.

"Ready," he said with a sigh.

John nodded and swung the carriage door open.

Adam turned to Swinton. "Let's go. I won't be coming back."

The barest flash of pain cut behind Swinton's stoic eyes. "As you wish, Your Grace."

Devil take it. Adam's heart twisted as he stared back at his butler in belated realization. Swinton would do whatever he was told, even if it meant leaving the woman he cared about behind. The stubborn codger was loyal to a fault. Adam swallowed the tight lump in his throat.

"I can't ruin both our lives." He gestured at the open cottage door. "Stay."

Swinton's voice was stern. "I've looked after you since you were a child, Your Grace. I won't stop now. If you go, we both go."

They went.

CHAPTER 16

*S*leep was impossible. Staying awake wasn't any better. Carole missed Adam, missed her sketchbook, and had missed the perfect chance to explain to him that the reason she'd said no wasn't because she didn't care about him, but because she *did*.

Would it have made any difference? Probably not. Thoughts of her would vanish the moment he was back in the beau monde, surrounded by aristocratic beauties who could offer endless things that Carole could not. She slumped atop her writing desk. No matter who he married, she would always be the first one to love him for who he was.

None of this had been a game. She couldn't let him leave without a proper goodbye.

Leaving Judith to sleep in for another hour or two if she could, Carole ran out of her house without bothering with her hair or the wrinkled state of her day dress, and banged upon Adam's door with the knocker.

And banged.

And banged.

It wasn't until a sleepy-eyed young footman opened the door that she realized coming to call at nine o'clock in the morning after a party that had ended at dawn wasn't exactly the best idea she'd ever had.

"Adam," her mouth blurted. "Is His Grace awake?"

"I couldn't say, Miss." The footman stared back at her, his expression blank. "He isn't here."

Not... here?

"He went into town at *this* hour?" she asked in disbelief. "Where in the world would he—"

Not. Here.

"Gone?" She whispered to the footman.

He nodded. "I'm afraid so, miss. Left for London a couple hours ago."

"When will he return?" She regretted the question as soon as it was out of her mouth. Of course the footman wouldn't know the answer.

He shook his head. "Never, Miss. He took what he cared about, and said he wouldn't be back."

A blade of regret sliced through her, jagged and searing.

She'd always believed that the best thing about being a dedicated spinster was never risking the pain of loss. Not ending up like her father. But she *did* lose. Without even having the years of bliss first.

This was her fault. Not Adam leaving; they'd both always known it would come to that. But he didn't have to leave so suddenly. With so many things unsaid between them.

"Miss?"

"Thank you," she mumbled. "I didn't mean to rouse you from slumber." She started to turn away, then thought better of it. "When you speak to Swinton, can you ask him—"

"Can't, Miss." The footman made an apologetic face. "Left with His Grace, Mr. Swinton did."

Carole stared at him in horror, her heart beating too fast. She'd ruined Judith's chance at happiness as well as her own. This was going to destroy her.

Just as it was destroying Carole. There was nothing left for her here.

Somehow, she stumbled down Adam's front walk and back into her bedchamber. She shut the door firmly, crawled up into her fourposter bed, and closed the curtain tightly.

Darkness. That was what she needed. And

her pillow. And a good cry. But the tears didn't come, no matter how long she lay there, staring blindly into the dark. They didn't come until Judith crawled in beside her and said it wasn't Carole's fault. Sometimes people leave, even when we love them. Sometimes they leave and never come back. That was life. All they could do was carry on.

The days blended together. Carole stayed in her dark hideaway where it was safe. Where she could pretend she was still dreaming and might wake up at any moment.

The rattle of a tea tray jerked her back to the present. She waited in silence for the sound of the tray sliding onto the table and the metallic latch of the door, indicating Rhoda had returned to her duties. The tray rattled onto the table. The door did not close behind the maid.

Carole slipped a finger in the crack between her curtains and gasped.

Her father sat on the dressing stool next to the tea tray.

"What are you doing?" she stammered.

He poured two cups. "You didn't keep our billiards match."

A hitch somewhere between a laugh and a sob tangled in her throat. That was what it had taken for her father to take an interest in her life.

"Did you wait long?" she asked bitterly.

"Two days." He stirred a lump of sugar into one of the cups. "But I'm getting better at making your tea how you like it. Do you want some while it's still hot?"

Father had been bringing in her tea trays?

"I..." was all she managed.

He tied the curtains to the posts, then brought two steaming teacups to the edge of the bed. "Sit with me?"

She sat up and accepted the warm cup. "You forgot the saucers."

"I'm not very good at this," he answered lightly, but his eyes were full of pain. "I'm *not* good at this, love. I haven't been good at anything since your mother died."

Her heart twisted. "I've been trying to help. I—"

"You've been singlehandedly running this household since before you were old enough to leave the schoolroom. In my grief, I let you. I shouldn't have. I closed myself away when you needed me most."

"I didn't mind helping," she whispered.

"That's how you dealt with *your* grief. If you personally filled the hole, then maybe there wouldn't be one. Being in charge gave you a purpose. Making decisions about the menu made you feel you still had some say over life. I know, because I was doing the same thing, up in my study. I couldn't save your mother, but maybe I could save more money for our household. I just had to re-search a little more. Sell this stock. Buy that bond. Concentrate on the market."

She stared down into her cup and nodded. "I knew you were working."

"I wasn't working, sweetling. I was run-ning away. I was hiding inside ledgers and books and numbers. Sound familiar?"

"Maybe." Sketchbooks, billiards. Geometry she could predict. Drawings she could con-trol. "So what do we do?"

"We stop running away and start running *to*. That's why I came here to you." He tucked a strand of hair behind her ear. "What do *you* want?"

What she couldn't have.

"The duke next door?" Father guessed, his gaze fierce. "If he hurt you—"

"He asked me to marry him," she blurted. "I said no. He doesn't really want me. I'm not duchessy enough."

Father frowned. "What do duchesses do that you can't?"

"I don't know. They organize parties and decorate homes and manage households..." At her father's smug expression, she clarified, "*big* ones. For important people."

"Did he mean it?" Father asked. "When he asked you to marry him?"

She sighed. "It doesn't matter. He left."

"You said no," Father reminded her. "Maybe he needed a moment to hide, too. No one is perfect, love. Nothing ever is. But when it's right for *you*... say yes."

"It's too late," she said dully. "He's in London by now, with a gaggle of debutantes quacking at his heels."

Father's lips quirked. "I can't imagine you quacking."

"I missed my chance to find out," she said with a little shrug.

"Did you?" He rose to his feet and lifted a folded square of parchment from the tray. "Seems to me, your Great-Aunt Murray invites you to London every Season."

"I can't go," she stammered. "You need me here."

"You needed to be here," he said softly. "You tried so hard to be useful that you never noticed when you turned into the most capable young lady England has ever seen. If you want to go to London, you have my blessing. Do what your heart tells you."

"In that case..." Hope began to blossom. She hooked her arm through her father's. "You and Judith are coming with me."

CHAPTER 17

Carole rolled back her shoulders and stepped into a magnificent Mayfair town house. Mrs. Sands, the owner of the town house, was bosom friends with her great-aunt Murray.

Mrs. Sands had also landed the enviable coup of having the most eligible bachelor on the Marriage Mart accept her invitation to tonight's soiree.

Carole and Aunt Murray were running late. Judith had spent no less than an hour curling and pinning and arranging Carole's hair. She'd told her maid not to bother, that by now he'd have a dozen paramours.

"Not anymore," Judith said when she finally let her out the door.

But now that she was here, in the grandest residence she'd ever seen, surrounded by the crème de la crème of High Society, Carole once again felt like the green country girl she'd always been. How was she meant to compete with elegant ladies dripping in jewels and draped in the latest fashions?

She forced one foot in front of the other anyway. Maybe he wouldn't be there. Maybe coming all this way was all for nothing.

Maybe he'd be here, and refuse to acknowledge her in front of his fancy peers.

"Fetch me a lemonade, dear, would you?" her great-aunt asked.

By herself? Panic rushed through her, causing her knees to tremble. At home, Carole knew everyone. Here, she knew no one. Worse—here, she *was* no one. But her aunt was thirsty and Carole owed her everything for her hospitality, so she rolled back her shoulders and pretended not to feel like a crow among swans as she made her way to the refreshments table.

The Season wouldn't start for months, so at least she could only embarrass herself in front of the minimum quantity of people. Of elegant, rich, well-connected—

The familiar *snick* of ivory balls colliding caught her attention, and her gaze jerked toward an open doorway. Inside the adjoining room was a beautiful billiard table. A dozen spectators cheered on two impeccably dressed gentlemen.

Adam.

He adjusted his stance, lifted his cue, and delivered a perfectly competent cannon.

His opponent murmured something that made Adam laugh. Adam responded by saying something that made the three young ladies cooing behind him erupt into giggles.

Carole's fingers dug into her clammy palms. She did not belong. What was she doing here?

But as she turned to go, Adam's eyes met hers from the other side of the billiard table.

He froze half-stretched across the table, caught in the middle of positioning a shot. *"Carole?"*

"I need to talk to you," she managed. Or tried to. She wasn't certain the hoarse creak of her voice traveled loud enough for him to hear.

Adam handed his cue to one of his friends. He walked around the table to the doorway, but did not step into the main room. "What are you doing here?"

She took a deep breath and met him at the threshold. They would be seen, but not overheard.

"You don't have to say anything back," she said quickly, "but I can't leave things how they were without telling you the truth. And the truth is… I wanted to say yes, but I was terrified. I knew you meant it in the moment, but I also knew you'd come back to—" She gestured around them. "—*this*, and realize your mistake. I didn't want to be that mistake. I love you too much to spend the rest of my life knowing I was never truly good enough."

There. The words were out. She held her breath.

"I found your sketchbook," he said quietly.

Heat blazed her cheeks. "I... er..."

"I don't know what to say because I never do seem to have the right words. But I do have this." He slid his hand inside his waistcoat and pulled out her sketchbook.

Her mouth opened wordlessly. He'd been carrying around her sketchbook.

"Here." He teased out a folded sheet of foolscap he appeared to have been using as a bookmark. "I started working on it the day you agreed to help me find the perfect woman."

With trembling fingers, she opened the paper.

Required Qualities for my Future Wife

She glanced up. He motioned for her to keep reading.

Friendly
Fearless
Good with children
Must <u>like</u> each other!!
Honest
Reciprocates feelings
Thoughtful
Puts family first
Knows what she wants
Does everything she can to achieve it
Even though she doesn't need me... still wants me.

"*Those* are the only characteristics I care about." He took her hands in his and pressed them to his chest. "I modeled them after the perfect woman. *You.*"

Six months later

$\mathcal{A}$dam leaned his cheek against his wife's soft hair as they cuddled close for warmth in the outdoor seats of Cressmouth's bustling amphitheater. The annual Christmas performance of Shakespeare's *The Winter's Tale* was about to begin.

After having spent the months after their wedding nestled up north in their cottage, he'd miss moments like these in this cozy village when they returned to London for the parliamentary session.

On the other hand, Adam was looking forward to sharing a different kind of Season with Carole. Not just because she loved to research with him—her analytical talents meant he could finish work much faster, with more time to spend with each other.

That was what he was really looking forward to: introducing her to all the sights and tastes of London, waltzing with her anywhere they found an orchestra, challenging their friends to a memorable game of billiards...

It was hard to believe that when he'd first set eyes on his father's completely rearranged library, his instinct had been to throttle whoever had dared lay a finger on his cherished books. Instead, when he and Carole had discovered that the culprit was Adam's friend Theo while he was recuperating from his battle injuries, Adam could have kissed him and thrown him a parade for helping bring him and Carole closer together.

He and Carole weren't the only ones to benefit. Adam glanced over the top of Carole's head to grin at the couple seated on her other side. Now that Swinton and Judith lived in the same household, there was no longer any reason for them to have to sneak away to hide their attraction. In fact, they were *both* Swintons now, having called the banns the month after Carole and Adam's wedding.

Carole's father was coming out of his shell more and more. Instead of exiting his study once a week, the Azurefords and the le Ducs had joined forces to create the first annual

Cressmouth billiard tournament—with Mr. Quincy as captain.

Adam nuzzled his wife's hair. "If you could sketch anything you pleased into this moment, what would you change?"

"Nothing at all." She smiled up at him. "What would you change?"

"I'd add *this*," he said, and lowered his mouth for a kiss.

THE END

~

What happens when Désirée le Duc becomes the appallingly unqualified governess to twins Annie and Frederick... and finds herself falling for their roguish father?

Join the fun in *The Duke's Bride*, the next romance in the *12 Dukes of Christmas* series!

THANK YOU FOR READING

Love talking books with fellow readers?

Join the *Historical Romance Book Club* for prizes, books, and live chats with your favorite romance authors:
Facebook.com/ groups/HistRomBookClub

Check out the *12 Dukes of Christmas* facebook group for giveaways and exclusive content:
Facebook.com/groups/DukesOf-Christmas

Join the *Rogues to Riches* facebook group for insider info and first looks at future books in the series:
Facebook.com/groups/RoguesToRiches

Check out the **Dukes of War** facebook group for giveaways and exclusive content:
   Facebook.com/groups/DukesOfWar

And check out the official website for sneak peeks and more:
   www.EricaRidley.com/books

ACKNOWLEDGMENTS

As always, I could not have written this book without the invaluable support of my critique partner, beta readers, and editors. Huge thanks go out to Erica Monroe and Tessa Shapcott. You are the best!

Lastly, I want to thank the *12 Dukes of Christmas* facebook group, my *Historical Romance Book Club,* and my fabulous street team. Your enthusiasm makes the romance happen.

Thank you so much!

ABOUT THE AUTHOR

Erica Ridley is a *New York Times* and *USA Today* best-selling author of historical romance novels.

In the new *Rogues to Riches* historical romance series, Cinderella stories aren't just for princesses... Sigh-worthy Regency rogues sweep strong-willed young ladies into whirlwind rags-to-riches romance with rollicking adventure.

The popular *Dukes of War* series features roguish peers and dashing war heroes who return from battle only to be thrust into the splendor and madness of Regency England.

When not reading or writing romances, Erica can be found riding camels in Africa, zip-lining through rainforests in Central America, or getting hopelessly lost in the middle of Budapest.

～

Let's be friends! Find Erica on:
www.EricaRidley.com

Printed in Germany
by Amazon Distribution
GmbH, Leipzig

25969388R00117